TORN APART

Twisted Killer Series

SterlingHouse Publisher, Inc.　　Pittsburgh, PA

Other titles in
The Twisted Killer Series
The Maze Murderer
Tainted Blood
Black Ribbon

TORN APART

Perothrillers

ISBN-10: 1-56315-398-X
ISBN-13: 978-1-56-315398-3
Trade Paperback
© Copyright 2010 Charles Pero
All Rights Reserved
Library of Congress #2009922483

Requests for information should be addressed to:
SterlingHouse Publisher, Inc.
7436 Washington Avenue
Pittsburgh, PA 15218
info@sterlinghousepublisher.com
www.sterlinghousepublisher.com

Pero Thrillers
is an imprint of SterlingHouse Publisher, Inc.

Cover Design: Brandon M. Bittner
Interior Design: Kathleen M. Gall
Images provided by iStockphoto.com

All rights reserved. No part of this publication may be reproduced, stored in a retrieval system, or transmitted in any form or by any means...electronic, mechanical, photocopy, recording or any other, except for brief quotations in printed reviews...without prior permission of the publisher.

This is a work of fiction. Names, characters, incidents, and places, are the product of the author's imagination or are used fictitiously. Any resemblance to actual events or persons, living or dead, is entirely coincidental.

Printed in U.S.A.

DEDICATION

To my nieces and nephews,
Priscilla, Adriana, Peter V, Erica, Frank, Anthony, Dea, John,
Kaci, Joey, Gianna, Frankie, Giovanina, and Christina.
I love you and wish you all
a future of love, peace and harmony.

PROLOGUE

"U R DEAD!"

The black letters stood out against their white background, chilling in their implication, brilliant in their simplicity. Without a sound, the six capital letters screamed out into the silence of his cramped dorm room.

Alex Ritchey read the text message on his computer screen and scoffed. He waited a beat for the inevitable follow-up message, and then smiled when it popped up just below the original: "IF U DON'T START STUDYING—RIGHT NOW!!"

He began typing, but was only halfway through his reply when another message popped up on his screen: "I MEAN IT!" came the terse demand, followed shortly by a caveat: "TURN OFF THE PORN & HIT THE BOOKS!!!"

He blushed, quickly logged off, and shut down the cyber porn site he'd been cruising instead of studying for his upcoming Sociology mid-term. Hey, who could blame a guy? When the choice was Laslow's hierarchy of needs or www.Need-2-Screw.com, the typical college freshman literally had no choice; it was cyber porn all the way.

Expecting the inevitable knock any second, he turned his back to the now-dark computer screen, propped his feet up on his bed, and cracked open the approximately 3,000-page Sociology text to an indiscriminate page. Right on cue, her soft knock announced a quick entrance.

"Caught you!" she smiled, dashing over to his work station

on long, coltish legs that fairly whispered against her tight, pink gym shorts. He didn't need to look to know that big white letters spelled the word C-H-E-E-R across her firm backside. Her white tank top shared the same legend, the five pink letters spelling out "CHEER!" stopping just above her flat, bare midriff.

"No way!" he scoffed, quickly trying to close the book before she could mark his place. Too late; a long, polished finger darted between the closed covers just as he slammed them shut. With a strength that never failed to surprise him, Mandy Collins, she of the capital letter fetish and psychology major, whisked the book from his hands to declare, "Aha! Chapter 16. Too bad our exam only goes up to Chapter 12, smart guy."

Alex smirked her favorite smirk, knowing it would melt her into a pile of gooey warm fuzzies. He was not disappointed. "I know you think you can breeze through your mid-terms, smart guy," she oozed, her long thigh edging perilously close to his own, "but don't forget what your father said. Anything less than a 3.7 average and he'll cut you off. And we don't want that, now do we, honey bunny?"

Alex blushed. Mandy was no gold-digger—combined, her hoity-toity Manhattan legal-eagle parents were worth almost as much as his own father—but they'd both grown accustomed to living the high-life at the tony private university nestled in the foothills of Schenectady. Bryson College wasn't exactly a party school, but with their combined allowance, the two had managed to do their best to turn it into one. The last thing Alex needed was another hit to his wallet.

The mention of his father caused his handsome face to grow churlish as he spat, "You let me handle my old man. I can pull a 3.7 in my sleep, baby, you know that."

"I know that," she cooed, sitting down on his bed and poking a finger playfully into his knee. "I'm just not sure your professors are as convinced. Or your counselor, or the registrar's office, or the admissions department, or...."

"I get the point," he said, smiling as she pulled his pillow over to cover her perfect stomach. Even with a figure most girls would die for, Mandy was painfully insecure. The sincerity of her plea, the doting look in her eyes, made his heart stir.

"Okay, okay," he sighed, giving her his serious look. "I'll get back to studying, Mandy. Promise. Just as soon as I brush up on my Human Anatomy 101, that is."

He reached for her thigh, but like a shot she had already rocketed halfway across the room. "Nice try, pretty boy," she gurgled, her breathy voice sounding like bubbles escaping a fine bottle of champagne. "I've got to study too, you know. You bring me a 3.7 G.P.A. tomorrow, Big Boy, and I'll let you tap this Grade-A piece of A.S.S. Deal?"

As the door swung shut in her wake, he could hear her giggling all the way down the hall. Alex Ritchey sighed, yet another victim of freshman blue balls, and turned at last to his studies. An honor student with an impeccable pedigree, he was no stranger to studying, but like many to whom good grades came easily, he considered it the ultimate insult. Still, the thought of Mandy's firm flesh pressed against his own in less than 24 hours was an excellent motivator, and so he was surprised when, two hours and three chapters later, a heavy hand began knocking on his door.

Alex rubbed his study-bleary eyes and glanced at the digital clock by his bed. The glowing red numbers read 1:12 a.m. "What the...!" he grumbled as he stood up, stretched, and limped across the floor on legs still half-asleep. "Who is it?" he asked, staring at his roommate's Marilyn Manson poster on the back of their dorm room door.

"Pizza!" came the sharp reply.

Alex grinned. "What? Again?" Such was dorm life. At least two nights a week, if not more, the clueless pizza delivery boy knocked on the wrong door. Alex, who always kept a spare twenty handy on just such occasions, had been the lucky recipient of more than his share of unordered pizzas lately. Tonight, however, he was eager to get some sleep and quickly opened the door to direct the pizza boy to the right room number.

"I didn't order…" was all he was able to manage as a large shape shoved him back in the room. Alex barely had time to notice the color of the uniform or the name on the pizza box as he was shoved back toward his bed. The shape never let up. It was like standing in the path of a Mac truck. Alex fought against it, but time and time again his young, balled fists landed on the solid ground of a hard, cold chest as he was shoved inexorably backward.

Only when Alex stumbled backward onto the bed did he notice the large, fleshy arms, the bright, gold watch, and the pizza-dough-free T-shirt that hid the barrel chest he'd been pounding in vain. This was no pizza boy; it was a man. And unless Tony Soprano had started delivering for Dominoes, it wasn't exactly pizza he was delivering.

"What the…!" he repeated, just before a fist slammed mercilessly into his face, rendering him senseless, if not exactly unconscious. He vaguely recalled an empty pizza box landing beside his bleeding lips as his world spun around him. There was no time for action, no time for thought.

Alex, who had watched a hundred or more karate movies in his young life and had always considered himself a student of the art, had no spirit left after the first punch landed. All those hours in the gym, all those curls and reps, all those moves he'd learned on the wrestling team at his old prep school, failed him miserably.

Towering above him, the man stood poised to deliver a repeat performance. From Alex's position, the nameless, faceless man might as well have been the Jolly Green Giant, bent on his destruction at any cost.

Alex was disgusted to hear a whimper escape from his throat, and doubly so when a look of grim satisfaction passed across the man's thick, fleshy face. The burp of a walkie-talkie or cell phone blared in Alex's ringing ears, but as he danced on the border of consciousness, he could only make out snatches of conversation while the man barked nearly indecipherable phrases into his sleek phone:

"…out like a light…."

"…construction chute…."

"…pissed his pants…."

"…just like we planned…."

Through the haze of pain, wondering whether or not his father would make him pay for his own reconstructive surgery, Alex focused on only two words as the man spoke: construction chute.

All month long they'd been renovating the dorm rooms, one by one. Downstairs was a concrete splattered Dempsey dumpster, full of old student desks and broken chairs. Alex and his roommate had been daring each other all week, saying that, once the serpentine construction chute that led straight down to the dumpster finally made it to their window, they'd guzzle a six-pack of Heineken each and then slide down to see what all the fuss was about.

Just that morning the chute had mysteriously popped up outside their window—a week ahead of schedule—but Alex's roomie Paul was still back home, straightening out a DUI he'd gotten over the summer.

"Lucky him," Alex grumbled through bloody lips already

starting to swell and crack. His teeth felt loose, but he was fairly certain his nose was okay.

"What's that, pretty boy?" barked the big man with the fat fist. "Come on then, no time for chit-chat. You're going for a ride, Ivy League. Lucky you, indeed; my friends will be at the bottom waiting for you. Don't worry, I'll catch up with you shortly. We've got big plans for you, frat boy, big plans indeed."

With that, Alex Ritchey was hoisted off his bed and dragged over to the window. Only when he saw the long, blue chute affixed to his ledge did he finally start to panic. The gaping black hole looked barely big enough for him to squeeze through, let alone slide down, and the sight of it shocked him back to reality. He was not going into the chute. Not now, not ever. With a strength that surprised him, he pulled free from the big man and made a mad dash for the door.

He lunged across the room, his running shoes finding purchase on the clothes-scattered floor. Behind him lumbered the big man, his tight pizza delivery shirt straining against his massive chest. Alex beat him to the door, but the blow must have knocked his equilibrium off. Reaching for the door handle felt like an exercise in stupidity. He could find it, but had trouble turning it.

Just as he finally got his right brain to send a signal to his left hand,—or was it vice versa?—the fat man in the tight shirt launched himself toward Alex's back with all the speed and force of a runaway train. The college freshman heard more than one rib break as the two collided, though he managed to remain conscious. At least until blood started gurgling from his nose.

Poor kid, he was going to miss the ride down the chute after all....

1

Frank Logan thumbed through a week-old issue of *Time* and tried hard not to feel like a piece of leftover meatloaf. Smooth jazz oozed from the tiny Bose stereo on the windowsill, some slow saxophone riff that sounded like all the other slow saxophone riffs he'd heard since opening up shop at 8 that morning.

He sighed, and replaced the well-thumbed news magazine back on the reception table, taking the time to make sure to carefully fan the magazines out just so. He stood up from the overstuffed leather chair poised next to the well-fed ficus plant in the reception area and stretched his back, digging both sets of knuckles into the softening flesh at the small of his spine.

God, he was getting old.

For perhaps the twelfth time that day, Frank wandered from his outer office back to the inner. It wasn't a long walk, maybe twenty feet all told, but at least it was a diversion from the grim routine of watching the entire day pass by without any human contact. The walls of his new office were thin, and he could hear the painful jazz solo in his inner office as loudly as he had in his outer sanctum.

That's what he got for sending his receptionist, computer programmer, Girl Friday, and DJ home early. Dana was a doll, and had a hell of a figure to boot, but hearing her yap on the phone with the rest of the gals from the office complex secretarial pool was worse than 5,000,000 sax solos at once.

By lunch he'd had enough and, God love her, she hadn't demurred when he offered her a half-day instead of a full. As she gathered up her oversized leather purse and filled it with her clattering keychain collection to head off for the long weekend, he'd been tempted to follow her, maybe catching a matinee at the multiplex down the street or even getting a jump on happy hour down at Bernie's Bar on 4th and K Streets. But he was a Bureau man through and through, and that meant staying till business hours were over, whether you were painfully slow or dreadfully busy.

Frank cringed upon entering his inner sanctum, suddenly reminded of why he spent so much time in Dana's domain in the first place. For there, on the walls, was his gallery of book covers, from his very first to his very latest, expertly framed and blown up to at least ten times their original size. Interspersed were smaller frames picturing his face on a dozen or more magazine covers, as well as a select grouping or two of his more notable newspaper headlines.

He tried to avoid them as he paced from door to desk and back again, but it was impossible to do so. They were everywhere: over the water cooler in the corner and the file cabinet against the wall, above his desk and across from his desk and beside his desk and on the other side of his desk. It was like being in a museum, only he wasn't dead yet. Although he had to admit that, on days like these, he felt pretty close.

It had seemed like the logical interior design move at the time. His longtime publisher, Doubletree Press, provided them gratis, and they'd been lying around in his garage for years now. Why not put them to some good use and, if seeing a wall of his latest bestsellers convinced a hesitant client to sign on the dotted line, so be it.

Of course, that had been six months ago when he'd left

the Bureau and gone into business as a private investigator. License #X-3784QR7, thank you very much. If you looked hard enough between the book and magazine covers, you could see it there, framed on the wall, just above the thermostat.

At first, getting his PI license and setting up shop in the newest office building on the Beltway (well, a tad off the Beltway, to be precise, but at least the way was clearly visible, from the top floor, on a sunny day) seemed like a no-brainer. The reviews for his latest book were great, and he'd left the Bureau with over 30 years in and at the top of his game. He'd left his old partner, Vinny Smalldeano, behind to be his eyes and ears, a loyal source inside the department should the need for quality inside information ever arise.

Leaving his old life behind had been easier than he thought. After all, Frank had grown tired of the inter-office politics and the not-so-subtle hints that he was "using the Bureau" to feed his own "publicity machine," at least in the words of a none-too-subtle performance review just before Frank pulled the plug. To quell the controversy and prove the naysayers wrong, he'd done the unexpected and walked away from a nearly 35-year career to start all over as a PI.

It might have been the oldest story in law enforcement, but Frank was hardly your typical PI. For one thing, he didn't need the money. Even if he never wrote another word—or sold another book—he had more than enough money to retire and live more than comfortably, several times over if the truth be told.

No, the PI gig was just to keep from going insane while pacing from one end of his exclusive Georgetown brownstone to the other. He figured he'd invest in a fancy espresso machine, get one of those mini Bose sound systems, tune into a classical station, catch up on his reading, and spend his time in between consulting for Court TV and CNN, looking for the occasional true crime case for his next book.

Once he'd invested the time and effort in getting the license and renting the office suite, though, he'd slowly warmed to the idea. Obviously, Frank's undercover days were over. From his salt and pepper gray hair to his trademark scowl, he was about as incognito as Paris Hilton at a nightclub opening.

Surveillance, he supposed, was out of the question, too. Years of daylong stakeouts in cramped quarters had left him with a bladder the size of a walnut and bad knees to boot. But that hadn't stopped a steady stream of wannabe clients knocking on his door those first few, heady months. In the beginning, everybody had wanted a piece of the Frank Logan mystique. (That half-page ad in the *Washington Post* hadn't hurt things, either.)

Although his first dozen or so clients paid him exorbitant fees to track down cheating wives or deadbeat dads, Frank got the feeling they were more interested in telling their friends who their PI was than actually getting the results he worked so long and hard for. It bothered him a bit at first, but he knew these were just the rubber neckers and gadflies. Once the shine wore off and the dust settled, the *real* clients would come around. The tough cases.

Missing persons.
Cold cases.
Unsolved murders.
The good stuff.

Well, the shine was off and the dust had settled, and his doorway was still empty. The reporters who'd announced his grand opening with such pomp and circumstance weren't returning any of his phone calls, his new agent was hinting around that the numbers for his latest paperback release were "more than disappointing," and most days he and Dana passed the full 8 hours with nary a phone call or door knock. He'd caught up on all his reading, switched from classical to jazz, and traded in that Crate and Barrel espresso-maker for a good old Mr. Coffee.

And here it was, another Friday, three in the afternoon, with another two hours to go before he could swing by the local deli and pick up a six pack and a roast beef grinder for the long, lonely night ahead. He sighed, listened to another sax solo from the outer reception area, and buried his head in his hands.

He was still sitting like that sixteen minutes later when the door to the outer office creaked open, startling him out of his midday nap. Instinctively he reached for his gun, then he realized it was safely locked in the top drawer of his desk and, besides, this wasn't a stakeout. This was his office. He stood up too abruptly, banging his knees on the underside of his fancy, newfangled desk, and then bruising his thigh as he cut the corner too fast and dinged himself a good one on the flat edge.

"Shit!" he grumbled, only to do a double-take as he rushed to the outer office and stared at a vaguely recognizable face. The oldish man with the trim physique and John Lennon glasses stared back at Frank and offered a greeting.

Kind of.

"Frank Logan?" he asked more than believed, an inquisitive twinkle in his sharp, hazel eyes. "*The* Frank Logan?"

"The indeed," Frank chuckled self-consciously, stifling the urge to give his intruder a bear hug. He still had a ways to go in the customer service department, but it had been so long since he'd handled a new client he was now swinging in the opposite direction, from grizzled, hardnosed veteran to smarmy salesman. Frank extended a hand, suddenly sweaty, and was surprised by the thin man's firm grip.

"Arthur J. Ritchey III," said the bespectacled gentleman, and suddenly Frank knew why his face looked so familiar. Glancing down to the coffee table reaching just to their knees, Frank spied Richie's face staring back at him from the cover of *Time*.

"THE Arthur J. Ritchey III?" Frank asked.

The man followed Frank's glance down to the magazine cover and grimaced. "God, I always hated that picture," he said with a sneer, quickly looking back up at Frank with eyes both wise and wary.

Frank realized they were still shaking hands and felt the man pull away abruptly, his aversion to close physical contact apparently as distasteful as his image on the cover of a magazine. Not too subtly, he wiped his palm on the leg of his fitted gray slacks. Frank blushed, feeling out of place and over solicitous. In his own office, no less. "It's an honor, sir," he said blandly, offering Ritchey a seat in the overstuffed chair beside the front door.

Ritchey sat daintily, as if afraid he might catch something, and looked around the claustrophobic outer office with a critical eye. Frank took a seat on the corner of Dana's desk, affecting a casual approach, as he'd seen cops do so often in the movies. All that was missing from his Bogart pose was a battered fedora hanging from the coat rack and an unfiltered cigarette smoldering at his side. "What can I do for you today, Mr. Ritchey?"

The man stared back blankly, then tapped the magazine cover for emphasis. "You mean you don't know why I'm here?" he asked.

Frank stared back with a blank look, a man unaccustomed to being surprised. "Should I?" he asked.

Ritchey barely concealed a snort as he shook his head. "I

see," he sighed. "So the magazines are just for show, is that it?"

Frank could have kicked himself. He was getting soft and moldy in the private sector. He'd picked up that same magazine a dozen times or more since it had arrived but had never bothered to read the cover story. What more did he need to know about Arthur J. Ritchey III? Everyone knew he was a successful international businessman, importing and exporting things Frank could hardly pronounce. Forbes list every year, down toward the bottom but, hey, still on the list. Friend of all the right people. Trophy wife. Donated just the right amount to all the right charities. What could *Time* tell him that the *National Enquirer* hadn't already?

"Perhaps it's better that you *don't* know the story beforehand, Mr. Logan," Ritchey reconsidered, eyeing Frank with a reserved indifference. "Maybe it's good you don't already know the sordid details. That way, you can look at the case with a fresh pair of eyes."

"Case?" Frank asked.

Ritchey nodded grimly, glancing around the room as if the walls of a former FBI agent's office might have ears. "It's my son," the powerful shipping magnate admitted. "He's gone missing, Mr. Logan. He was studying in his dorm room late last week, according to his girlfriend, and…just…vanished. Never showed up for his mid-term, stood her up for a date. His roommate found blood on the back of his door and his Sociology book lying in the middle of the floor. There was an empty pizza box on his bed and concrete dust on the windowsill. The campus police did a thorough search, the locals too, but nobody's seen him since."

A heavy silence filled the room. Frank waited, guessing there was more to the story. Bitter custody battle, hostile takeover, rival business partners, drug addiction, some extenuating circumstances that had brought Ritchey to a PI instead of the Feds. There wasn't.

Arthur J. Ritchey III looked up from his starched lap and said, "I saw you on the news a few months back. Heard you'd left the Bureau, hung up your shingle in the private sector. I've read all your books, Frank. May I call you Frank? Read them all, every last one. I know you're the best. I know you're expensive. I need the best, Frank, and I'm willing to pay for it. Can you help me?"

Frank nodded, resisting the urge to squeeze Arthur J. Ritchey III on his thin, slumped shoulder and thank him profusely for dragging him out of the doldrums. He didn't seem like a warm and fuzzy kind of guy. It also didn't seem like that kind of case.

Already Frank's head was reeling. Empty dorm room, hot girlfriend, pizza box, bloody handprint, daddy's boy, magazine covers, lots of pressure to succeed. Based on this initial rough sketch, Frank was fairly certain he'd find the boy holed up in some nearby crack den, owing a 400-pound drug dealer several grand and all too eager to apologize to Daddy when Frank rescued him from a grim fate.

"I can help you, sir," Frank pledged.

After all, he thought, *how hard could it be to find a pampered frat boy?*

2

Vinny Smalldeano had never gotten used to Frank Logan's old office. From the first day he set foot on such hallowed ground, it had just never felt...*right*. He didn't mind the accolades or the promotion, and he certainly didn't mind the leapfrog in pay grades, but there was just something dead wrong about taking over Frank's hallowed domain.

How many times had he sat in this very office, on the other side of that very desk, Frank chewing him out over this mistake or that missed clue? How many times had he knocked on the door, only to find Frank on the other side, schmoozing some senator or lobbyist, the happy Washingtonian strutting out with a signed copy of one of Frank's hardcover bestsellers and a cocky grin on his face?

Now he was supposed to walk in Logan's footsteps? It was hard enough taking the practical jokes and well-meaning asides from their mutual colleagues. If he never heard, "How ya doing, Mr. Logan? Er, sorry, make that Mr. Smalldeano," again he'd be a very happy man.

Still, he couldn't complain. Taking over the Special Circumstances unit from the one, the only, Frank Logan was an honor few could boast of. Feeling like he deserved it was doubly satisfying. And so it was with some relief that Vinny drank in the office scuttlebutt about "big changes" coming down from the top brass.

Vinny, it was rumored, was due for another move. No one

could say whether the move was horizontal or vertical, but as far as Vinny was concerned, anywhere but Frank's old office would be a welcome trip he'd be more than willing to take.

Vinny was profiling a series of special circumstances killings taking place in New Mexico when Margie Holcomb, Frank's old assistant, popped her head full of vibrant red hair into his office and said, "Senior Director Flaherty is here to see you, Mr. Smalldeano."

Vinny knew he was in for it whenever Margie called him by his full name, but her face was deceptively noncommittal as she led in the fabled FBI Director. Long and lean, looking a third of his seventy years if not half that, Flaherty was rumored to be on the short list for the head slot at the Bureau, and looked like he was already being groomed to sit across from the President and accept the position.

"Smalldeano my boy," Flaherty boomed in his Irish-tinged voice, "keep your seat, keep your seat. This is an unofficial visit, so there's no need to follow protocol, young lad."

Vinny knew no visit by a man as high-ranking as Flaherty was "unofficial," but he stood up nonetheless, reaching a well-muscled arm across his messy desk to take Flaherty's large hand into his own. "To what do I owe the honor today, sir? For this 'unofficial visit,' I mean."

Flaherty guffawed good-naturedly, pouring himself into the seat across from Vinny's desk. He had a roguish head of dirty blond hair and a face full of well-placed wrinkles he liked to call "laugh lines." His eyes were steely and bright, and his old Irish cop act wasn't fooling anyone. His pedigree was pure Beltway, and those who fell for his easy charm and aw shucks jive knew too quickly just how wrong they'd been when he slapped the cuffs on, as he'd done so often in his days as a DC beat cop God knows how many decades ago or, as in more recent years, when they found themselves transferred to Siberia for some grievance real or imagined.

"We're both busy men, Vinny," Flaherty said with a characteristic glance at his nondescript watch, "so I'll cut right to the chase. Ever since Frank left, your Special Circumstances squad has struggled to keep a high profile. This isn't news, right, Vinny? No need to answer. I know you're a smart boy and you know when I'm right. Right? To the point then: Tomorrow will come a decree from the top brass, myself included, recommending that funding for the Special Circumstances squad be cut drastically. Now, before you go getting all swarthy with your Mediterranean complexion there let me explain: The squad will survive on bare bones funding just long enough to clear your current caseload.

"Relieved, eh? Well, don't jump the gun there, kiddo. You, my friend, are being reassigned effective immediately. In light of recent terrorist activities overseas in Britain, France, etcetera, the funding from your old squad is to be funneled into a new squad, tentatively titled the International Elite. Ah, too right. I see the quizzical look on that swarthy face of yours. What, you're probably asking yourself right about now, is the International Elite squad? Don't worry, Vinny: your job description won't change. Only your location."

Flaherty let the bomb drop, then stay there. Vinny swallowed uncomfortably a few times in the deafening silence. Then, when he could stand it no more, he asked, "Sir?"

Flaherty smiled. "Breathe easy, son," he soothed, leaning forward in his chair conspiratorially and dropping his voice into a mellow, bourbon-soaked ooze. "This is the opportunity of a lifetime, my boy. You'll still be tracking killers, but as the name implies, you'll be doing it overseas. Just think of it, Vinny: England. Turkey. Russia. Ireland. Though I'm partial to that last, boyo. Think of it as a promotion *and* a relocation, all in one."

"But sir," Vinny interrupted. "How? I mean, isn't that what the CIA does?"

Flaherty gave him a stern look, but the junior agent got the feeling it was intended for the crimes, not the questioner. "Let's face it, son. We're at war. And not just with Iraq and Afghanistan. The whole world hates us. Yes, yes, even our allies would stab us in the back if they got the chance and thought the U.N. would look the other way. When we got the nod for Homeland Security, we were the recipients of a dozen tiny loopholes. Did I say a dozen? Make that *dozens*, Vinny.

"Frankly, we don't need the CIA anymore. An American commits a crime overseas, we send you, Vinny. The CIA might get wind of it and try to beat you to the punch, steal your thunder, so to speak, but you, my boy, will be in charge. You'll be handling Special Circumstances cases overseas. That's all. New job title, same job description. Congratulations, my boy. I'm looking at the new head of the new International Elite squad."

With that, Flaherty stood up; simple as that.

Meeting adjourned.

On his way to the door, the Senior Director turned around and, with a sparkle in his eye, said, "Don't worry if you missed anything, Vinny. This will all be in tomorrow's memo. By the way, you do have a passport, don't you? I have the feeling you might be needing it sometime soon."

With that, Flaherty was gone leaving Vinny alone in Frank's old office.

Soon it would be Vinny's old office, too....

3

Alex Ritchey lay slumped in the back of the van and rasped his last few ragged breaths. It was a sad, lonely, and, as far as Alex was concerned, damned undignified way to die. He did not see his life flash before his eyes. He did not feel a presence or a light or the whisper of his name issued by a soft, divine voice beckoning him home. He did not see angels or devils or, for that matter, very much of anything at all.

The warehouse outside was dark and sullen. He knew from staring out the back of the van earlier that morning that blacked-out windows along the roof occasionally let in a shaft of light if it struck just right, illuminating an abandoned building as big as his university campus.

There wasn't much inside the warehouse for him to look at, and his injuries were too grave for him to even consider sneaking out of the van and limping around the grounds to get a better look, like the hero might in a movie; his teeth white, his hair just so, his clothes terrifically un-bloodied and his wounds already forgotten by an audience merely waiting for the next explosion or digital effect. There were some big machines over here, some empty boxes over there, and an outdated soda machine whose oversized plug was clearly visible on the floor in front of its rusty, darkened hull.

But that had been hours ago—or was it days—when he had still had the strength to get up and move around his four-wheeled coffin. Those few, precious, stolen moments were long since gone.

Now it hurt just to breathe; moving was clearly out of the question.

The broken ribs, the twisted ankle and various scrapes and bruises and punctures and tears that had resulted from his unconscious ride down the construction tube had finally taken their toll. He chuckled to himself wryly, thinking how, if this had been a movie, Steven Segal or Van Damme or The Rock would have had a smile on his face the whole way down the tube, not a scratch on him, and kicked the asses of every bad guy waiting for him on the other end. So much for the reality of his highly-prized DVD collection.

Real life, it seemed, was not quite so painless. Now he lay in wait, but not for his captors—whom he hadn't seen in the last 24 hours—but the Grim Reaper, whom he was certain lurked just around the corner.

The van was cold and dark, the steel ribs of the bare floorboard biting into his own as they lay cracked and twisted to the point where he could feel them poking against the pale, bruised skin of his aching and bloody back. It was the same van that had been waiting at the foot of that concrete-stained tube, the same van in which he'd sprung to life in transit, the deep darkness outside worsened by the large, sweaty bodies surrounding him like so many running backs in one of his long-forgotten varsity football huddles.

He had been smart enough, or scared enough, to keep his eyes clenched shut, though it had been harder to stop himself from screaming at the intense pain that greeted him upon waking from his restless slumber. Around him the men had whispered harsh epithets and desperate demands, of which he'd heard only snatches:

"If he dies, what then?"

"We can still get the ransom. His old man will never know."

"...proof that he's alive. Maybe we should cut off a finger or toe?"

"All they'll need is DNA; we can get that from his hair or...."

Through the blood-soaked haze of his deafening pain, it had sounded just like the plot of a bad *Law & Order* episode. Although they never again laid another hand on him, the torture came in waves nonetheless. At times the pain was so intense it was like a living thing, speaking to him in the harsh language of marrow and bone, blood and twisted flesh. At other times it was blessedly quiet, whispering to him in muted tones that promised more to come.

In those times, when the pain had dulled and he could once again concentrate on his precarious position, he tried to make out his captors. There were several of them, their voices indistinguishable from one another but their shapes big enough, and numerous enough, to at least count.

Three. No, wait. Four? Five? He couldn't be sure. Though they were dressed in workman's uniforms or camouflage, ball caps or rolled up ski masks, they looked older, fleshier, more pampered than your average thugs. They belonged in business suits, not these costumes.

Hell, he thought at one point, *they look just like my dad!*

They spoke intermittently as the rutted surface of whatever hellish back road they'd chosen broke into his pain-free reverie; sometimes he could even hear the jagged edges of his ribs slicing through lung, liver, or skin.

When he was conscious and not blacked out from the excruciating pain, he heard scattered phrases. An offshore account here, a wire transfer there. A throwaway cell phone, an unmarked car, a drop-off point. It was every ransom cliché he'd ever heard before. Any minute he expected Mel Gibson and Rene Russo to pop up and give him a pep talk!

He knew that would never happen. There would be no one to save him. Not now; not ever. His girlfriend wouldn't miss him until after his exam, when she called to see how he'd done. His roommate wouldn't be back for days; his professors, his counselors, his RA barely even knew who he was.

And his dad? Forget it. If they were trying to get money out of him, well, they might as well try spinning his hair into gold. They'd have a better chance.

At last the spinning wheels of the kidnap van had found purchase on solid ground, and the blessed concrete ribbon of pavement meant he could stay conscious a little while longer. Shortly after they left the rutted road the van slowed and, with much grunting and cursing, two of the oversized men got out.

In the blinding flash of manmade light that met the sliding of the opening door he saw their silhouettes and realized they, like the fake pizza delivery man who'd burst into his room, were a little long in the tooth for this kind of hijinx. The strain on their sweaty, jowly faces was evident. So was their thinning hair, graying beards, and Rolex watches. As he was staring, the glint of the floodlights that suddenly bathed the van from outside must have reflected on his half-opened eyes. Meathead muttered something about "the kid coming to" and then quickly rectified the situation with another pounding from his leaden fist.

The next thing Alex knew he was alone, still in the back of the van, and coming to halfway through a violent, retching cough that spewed blood all over the front of his sweat-stained T-shirt. The effort sent a shockwave through his ravaged body and sent Alex right back into unconsciousness. He stayed there, give or take a minute or two, for most of the next day. When he came to again, the broken rib god, or maybe just the real God, had mercy on him, at least long enough for him to rise up on hands and knees and fumble around to the back of the van.

There, with tears streaming down his face and nausea threatening to overtake him, he saw the empty warehouse, the silent soda machine, and the fresh oil stains of one or more luxury cars that had no doubt been pulled up next to the van while he was out cold. Nearby was a card table on which rested some cell phones and paperwork, but he was too far gone by then to look anymore, let alone leave the van and do anything about what he'd just seen.

He slumped back onto the floor, wincing in pain, and shifted around until he found comfort, for lack of a better term, in his final resting place. Now he stared at the blank, white ceiling of the van hoping, praying for release. Not out loud, for it hurt too much, but silently, mournfully, steadily, in the murmuring babble that crowded his battered brain.

He'd never been religious and, with his torrid past full of wine, women, and song, could hardly hope for heaven, but he didn't care as long as the throbbing, dull, searing pain ended. It would. And soon. Of that he was positive.

He listened for the sound of engines revving or doors slamming or phones ringing or sweat dropping or men cursing or ransom delivering and knew for a fact that he would never hear another sound again, save for that of his ragged breathing and the blood steadily dripping from the corner of his mouth down into the puddle that had recently formed next to his head.

The men, whoever they were, were gone. Long gone. He sensed their complete and utter absence the same way he knew he'd lost enough blood that no life-saving measures could ever replace his essence, his spark.

There were no ties to bind his wrists or ankles, no duct tape across his mouth, and in a way this scared him more than his broken ribs or stained T-shirt or bloody, matted hair. It meant they knew he was so far gone that restraint would have been redundant.

It meant they knew what he knew; Alex Ritchey was not long for this world.

He lay alone, in the back of a sparse, cold, empty van in the middle of a sparse, empty warehouse and waited for the dull, silent seconds to tick by. At the moment he didn't hate his abductors, didn't hate his father, didn't hate his girlfriend or his roommate or the construction crew who'd moved that damned blue tube or the professor who'd scheduled the exam for which he was supposed to be studying or the family priest who would surely give his eulogy.

Who he really hated were the directors, the actors, the producers of all those stupid Hollywood movies he'd grown up watching over and over and over again. He cursed them and their predictable storylines and glitzy special effects and blue screens and trick harnesses and stunt doubles and false reality.

For hours now he'd been waiting for the cavalry to arrive. For some grizzled detective and his hunches to track him down. For some beautiful, blond rookie to find the warehouse address in some old phone book and put two and two together. For some down on his luck FBI agent to be passing by and just happen to notice the fresh tire tracks leaving the rutted road on which he was traveling for some reason unknown to the audience. Isn't that how these things were solved? Isn't that what Movies of the Week were made of?

He'd been bred on TV, spoon fed it ever since the day his

Guatemalan nanny realized it soothed him better than banana pudding or warm milk or a bedtime story read to him in her beloved but broken English.

That soft blue glare had calmed him when his father raged and his mother cried, when his girlfriends broke up with him because they realized he was a spoiled, immature brat, or his so-called buddies dumped him because they found out he wasn't due to inherit his trust fund until he turned 21.

All those TV cops, all those Hollywood endings, all those last-minute rescues…where were they now? Where were Sippowitz and Barney Miller and Kojak and Baretta now? Nowhere; that's where.

Same place as him; nowhere. He'd been abducted in the middle of the night by men he'd never seen before and no doubt would never see again. He'd been stuffed in an unmarked van while the rest of his dorm mates partied or studied or screwed or slept and not a soul, he was sure of it, not a single, solitary soul had seen his disappearance nor, for that matter, were they ever likely to miss him should he not return.

He had, quite literally, vanished.

And now he would die in a warehouse where it had been so long since someone visited, the soda machine still sold Tab and Fresca! He wondered who would find his body, wondered if his father would cry when they did, and as he was wondering, the tiny sliver of bone that had been slowly invading his left ventricle for the past three hours at last broke off and entered his blood stream.

In less than a minute it was all over.

Like the soda machine and Kojak, Alex Ritchey was dead.

4

It had been nine days since the bottom fell out of his world, and Philip Bronstein had spent five of them getting settled in a squalid apartment—scratch that, they called them "flats" over here in jolly old England—with a leaky ceiling, moldy wallpaper, and a piss-poor view of Piccadilly Circus. He mistakenly kept referring to it as "Piccadilly Square," partly because it enjoyed him to piss off the locals, but mainly because the blinking neon Coke sign across the street reminded him of Times Square.

London. Who'da thunk it? A loudmouthed kid from Brooklyn, and look at him now, hiding out from Johnny Law "across the pond," as they'd said a dozen times while he was waiting to board Virgin-Atlantic Flight #674 bound for Heathrow from Dulles airport a mere 96 hours before.

The room—make that the flat—had a bed, a nightstand, a bureau, and a real-life chamber pot, on account of the communal bathroom down the hall, which Philip rarely used because a.) he had a germ phobia thing going on and b.) a shy bladder and c.) he preferred to drain his weasel into those annoying one-liter Coke bottles they had in London and then toss them out the window at 3 a.m. at the hustlers and whores who strolled Regent Street at all hours of the day or night. It gave him great joy to watch the garishly-painted streetwalkers scatter like glitter as the bottle invariably burst, spraying them with a tepid, fizzy mist of day-old piss.

Sometimes they looked up and gave Bronstein the bird. Other times they cried in each other's arms. One time a girl puked. Most times, though, they simply wiped themselves off and got right back to work. Too bad Bronstein was no longer in a position to hire any of them; with that kind of moxy, his old company could have just about run itself!

Quite a leap from the 300-square-foot private bathroom of his corner office in downtown DC, but then again, it sure as hell beat the communal bathroom in federal prison he'd otherwise be sharing if anyone ever found out what he'd done to deserve a forced sabbatical in cheery old Londontown.

As he waited for his daily order from the Chinese takeout dive around the corner on Coventry Street, he mused over the last five days. Five days. A full business week. It was the longest "vacation"—and he used that term with tongue planted firmly in his fleshy cheek—he'd ever taken from SouthCom Digital, LLC, the Fortune 500 Corporation he ran with a little help from his close friends and fellow fugitives.

Five days with no email. No faxes. No stock market tickers or text messages or news clippings or those damn pink "While You Were Out" message slips his plump, petite secretary Rita was always bringing him. Five days and all he had was the damn BBC on the 18" black and white with the rabbit ears standing on the bureau across from the bed.

And what the hell good was that? Like a bunch of Brits cared about some B-rate, white-collar crime from the states. "The States," they said every time he dared to venture outdoors for another pack of cigarettes or liter bottle of soda from the corner market, where he tried in vain to count out the pounds for himself and instead had to rely on the cheeky—damn, he was even starting to think like they talked—counter girl to peel off the right-colored bills for him.

He stared out the window now, leaning against the paint-peeling wall in his little sitting room—one wobbly end table, one ratty chair, no couch—mesmerized as always by the neon signs across the street. If he never saw the words SANYO or TDK for as long as he lived, he'd be a happy man.

Still, the colors amazed him. The sheer brilliance, the absolute audacity of all that shameless marketing thrilled the hot-headed, red-blooded American still very much inside him. The lights poured into each other, creating a dazzling waterfall of shimmering radiance. If you stared long enough, you could see each of the colors individually, kind of like the way a picture in the newspaper, magnified long enough and hard enough, it was inevitably reduced to a hundred thousand tiny black and white dots.

He stared at the lights, gazed at them, admired them until at last the timid knock at his hollow door announced that dinner was served. He could smell the beef and broccoli and three extra egg rolls wafting from beneath the flimsy door, and brusquely handed the tiny Asian holding his grease-stained paper bag a fist-full of pounds and slammed the door before he could complain.

This meal, such as it was, was his only highlight in the long, endless days of his forced exile. Every day the same. Little did he know it would be his last. And not quite that, after all. For Philip Bronstein had barely bitten into his first egg roll when a slight puff of air proceeded a tinkling of glass before a bullet promptly pierced his skull, sending brain and wonton and scalp and tiny shrimp against the top of his chair.

Had he had time, or enough brain matter, left to look at the bullet's source, he would have seen the tiniest of holes in the middle of his grease-smeared window. With his skull as a backstop, the bullet had nestled comfortably in the backrest of the chair after doing its dirty work, not even clattering to the floor to alert the downstairs neighbors to possible foul play in the room of the waddling, cranky Yank from above.

Five short days, and already Bronstein's vacation was over.

5

The Sniper waited patiently for Bronstein's dinner order to arrive. In his job, after all, patience truly *was* a virtue. No reason to kill the fat louse before the delivery boy showed up, banging on the door and asking for his money and rousing the neighbors, not to mention a good deal of attention from Scotland Yard in the process.

For three days the Sniper had shadowed Bronstein, following just 48 hours after his departure from the States. He'd slept little along the way, catching a catnap down in the Tube when he could get away with it, but lurking in the shadows of Piccadilly Circus more often than not, staring up at the dimly lit rented apartment day after day, night after night, glaring away the cheeky young hustlers with one squinted eye while he kept a close lookout for the ever-present Bobbies with the other.

Like most over the hill white American men-slash-corporate-lackeys, Bronstein was a creature of habit. Always shuffling down the stairs for his cigarettes and soda at the same time every morning, always ordering take-out at the same time each afternoon, always tossing his urine bombs out the window at the same time every night.

The Sniper had expected as much. He didn't know much about the man, hadn't had time to do his usual background work, but what he knew fit the pattern; here was a guy who, back in the States, had no doubt had his private car drive him down the same street to the same restaurant for the same meal at the same time for lunch every day. Like clockwork, day in, day out, until even the most casual observer would have known his routine.

Stupid. Short-sighted. Careless. And, as far as the Sniper was concerned, just plain lazy. But what was he to expect from some sad-sack, limp-dick corporate criminal? What was he to expect from a man so scared of being located that he didn't dare leave his apartment for more than ten minutes at the same time each morning? He had never even looked past the blinking neon lights across from his squalid room to see the beauty of The Angel of Christian Charity's statue, winged and glinting golden in the evening twilight above the Piccadilly Circus memorial fountain. He had never taken in a play at one of the many theaters on Shaftbury Avenue, where the Sniper himself had ducked in to enjoy two hours of quirky British drama only the night before.

The Sniper was no philosopher, but for once he'd wished his future victims would enjoy their last few hours. As far as he could tell, Bronstein had simply existed for the last three days. He hadn't once seen him smile, although he often leered after one of his soda bottles exploded at 3 a.m. If only the Sniper could have warned him that these few hours would be his last, to enjoy them, to soak up all life had to offer.

But, of course, that would have defeated the purpose.

Hiding in plain sight. The Sniper liked that phrase. Not only for its poetry, but also for its bearing on the matter at hand. As he disassembled his sleek rifle, intending to dispose of the parts in several different townships along the way back to the airport, he could see the blinking of the neon sign beneath him, illuminating the starched blue workman's uniform he'd cadged from one of the wall pegs in the downstairs basement just that morning.

He'd at first thought, and rightfully so, that the neon would be an impediment to his vision. But a quick stop at the Gap store across the street had left him endowed with a thick turtleneck sweater and the latest style of wraparound shades. A little pricey for his taste, but what the hell.

Like Bronstein, he was on vacation, right?

With a little modification, the turtleneck had been turned into a halo just beneath his chin, shielding the blinking haze of neon from below. (It didn't hurt that he'd swiped the wire hanger from the department store, as well as the sunglasses.) And then? With the shades in place, he could clearly see the outline of Bronstein's porcine figure answering the front door and greedily shuffling over to his favorite spot in the sitting room for his evening snack.

What might have seemed like mercy from the Sniper—letting his victim get comfortable, even allowing him a bite of his beloved egg roll before the bullet turned his brain into an order of Moo Shu pork—had in fact been carefully planned. Like an expert mathematician or professional pool player, the Sniper had worked out the calculations just so, allowing for just the right wind current, placement, and even the angle of the light.

The caliber of his bullet was just high enough to pierce the window, explode Bronstein's head like a pumpkin falling from the Empire State Building, and come casually to rest in the back of his chair.

A slightly stronger bullet might have pierced the victim's head all right, but was just as likely to slice through the back of the chair and even plow through the thick drywall and cheap construction of the wall behind. A slightly weaker bullet might have pierced the glass but lost velocity—or even a sense of direction—on the way to the middle of Bronstein's forehead.

In that sense, it was less of a final meal for the victim and more of a final exam for the Sniper.

With little time to admire his work, the professional relinquished his prime spot atop the Coke sign and wound his way down the service entrance until, by the time he was at street level, his boyish book-bag contained only parts of the rifle with which he was so deadly efficient.

There was no enjoyment of the street scene as he walked, quickly but not too hastily, no taking in the nightlife or brushing off the hustlers. There was no celebratory drink at one of the many lively pubs that dotted the avenues, which fell away like the miles between his young, sprightly feet, nor even a dalliance with one of the many prostitutes, male and female, who called to him from not-so-dark alleys along his carefully chosen route.

Like Bronstein, the Sniper's vacation was already over.

Unlike Bronstein, however, his work had only just begun.

6

Vinny Smalldeano's liaison, as the newest member of the newly formed International Elite squad, was a ruddy bloke named Squire—that's it, just "Squire"—who, as far as Vinny could tell, was fond of two things and two things only: American cigarettes and English beer. The reason he knew of Squire's dually unhealthy proclivities was because the two had spent the last three hours together staring up at the neon sign from which it was believed Vinny's victim was shot.

Vinny was suffering a dual case of jet lag and nicotine poisoning, neither of which he was used to nor very fond of, and was frustrated to no end to be sitting in the middle of Piccadilly Circus, unable to tag a single clue or take a single note.

Despite his hefty raise and lofty title, his inch-thick credentials and swaggering Clint Eastwood, "ugly American" stance, Vinny was suffering from more than just jet lag; he was in investigative limbo. Despite Flaherty's assurances that he'd be given "carte blanche on the other side of the pond," he had neither the jurisdiction nor the clout to be a part of the present inquiry.

Vinny squinted his eyes through the smoke screen that hung, ever-present, in the claustrophobic pub in which they'd been stewing for the last 180 minutes and asked for the umpteenth time, "Squire, why is it that I can't investigate what everyone in England, including the barmaid and that fellow over there playing darts, considers the crime scene?"

"Right, here then," Squire mumbled in his thick English accent, a cigarette in one corner of his bold, brash lips and a healthy sheen of Guinness foam coating the other. "It's all about jurisdiction, right? You must have heard the word on the telly, eh? *Kojak*? *Hill Street Blues* and such, eh? So, Scotland Yard's got first jurisdiction, then the Quad 400, this new task force they set up after the subway bombings—you heard of them, haven't you?—and then, last on the list, old pal o' mine, is your agency, er, what's it called again?"

"The International Elite Squad," Vinny blurted for the tenth time in as many minutes, his eyes straining to take in all 5'6" of Squire's wiry frame in the smoky haze that hung above their crowded table for two.

Squire slapped himself on the knobby forehead and smiled a thick, English smirk full of tobacco stained teeth that leaned and knocked into each other like so many rotting headstones in a zombie movie. "Spot on, how can one forget such a floral bouquet of a squad as that, right, mate?"

Vinny could neither stop his feet from tapping nor the veins in his neck from bulging as he watched Squire order himself yet another dark, frothy pint. The barmaid returned straightaway and Squire grabbed the glass before she could set it atop the already soggy table. She slapped him on the back and grew sober as a judge when handing Vinny another club soda and lime, which he hadn't asked for but drained quickly.

He set the empty glass on the soggy, coaster-coated table and sighed, as much out of frustration as a ploy to blow some of the thick smoke from around his head; it didn't work.

Flaherty, his boss back at headquarters, had made the trip sound like a VIP event—the death of one of America's Fortune 500 darlings having been on the news for a solid 48-hours by the time Vinny finally got tagged for the job—but so far it was a scene straight out of a budget pub tour, complete with Igor as his tour guide. Vinny admired Squire's official get up, such as it was: an ash-covered black sweater bearing squirrelly insignia about the shoulders and a beer-stained I.D. badge showing a much younger, much more sober Squire hanging in faded plastic about his thick, veiny neck.

The man's face was a study in hues; salt and pepper whiskers giving a nice contrast to the various shades of red that flashed across his face, depending on the emotion, like a human lava lamp. His fingers were surprisingly long and feminine around his fat, wide pint glass, and when they weren't glowering up at the glowing red neon sign that was their own personal ground zero, his hazel eyes could be blinding, quick, and alert.

The two had met at Heathrow several hours earlier, where a slightly more sturdy and spry Squire had greeted him at the baggage queue bearing a handwritten sign that said, simply, "YANK."

Naturally, Squire had had a lot of takers, as American after American stepped off the commercial flight from Dulles, but he'd waved the typical tourists away with an impatient flash of his hand until he'd spied Vinny in his standard issue G-man suit and conspicuous federal badge. The two had shaken hands brusquely and Vinny had next been led on a fast-paced tour through the streets of London, riding shotgun in a decade-old Fiat in which Squire displayed daring feats worthy of many a Hollywood stunt driver. No slouch of a driver himself, Vinny had arrived white-knuckled and invigorated as his tour guide had spent the next fifteen minutes parallel parking in front of the pub in which they now sat.

They'd been there ever since.

Finally, the outdated cell phone into which Squire had alternately barked and begged every hour on the hour chirped out a weak signal. So weak, in fact, that Vinny had to point out to his host that it was ringing.

Squire nodded around a fresh drag off his Marlboro Light, apparently swallowed the smoke—Vinny rarely saw him exhale, at least not so one would notice in the already thick fog around their heads—and picked up the phone with a blunt "Eh?"

Vinny spent the next two minutes watching Squire squint and nod into the phone until at last he said a farewell "Eh" and stood up with a flourish, knocking three hours worth of coasters and ashes to the ground as he signaled the barmaid, the dregs of one last cigarette cascading down his thick black sweater.

"What's the damage, pet?" he asked the infatuated beer wench, who quickly prattled off a figure that, even to Vinny's dim understanding of the pounds system, seemed a six-pack shy of what Squire had actually consumed. It didn't stop his host from taking offense, as the two locals spent a full three minutes haggling until at last Squire produced a pocketful of wrinkled notes and passed them across to the smugly satisfied waitress.

"Ready?" Vinny asked at last, no longer trying to hide his disdain.

"Carry on, mate," Squire oozed, as if he'd been waiting on Vinny instead of the other way around.

Both men flashed their badges at the young, apple-cheeked Bobbies guarding the service entrance to the outdated building atop which Piccadilly Circus's most famous landmark blinked 24 hours a day, 7 days a week. The two men seemed to know Squire by reputation, if not intimately, and with a practiced eye Vinny noticed them giggling in their wake.

Vinny felt a twinge of emotion for the first time all day,

and as the two climbed up flight after flight of narrow steps, he wondered how he might have felt if he were assigned to what basically amounted to babysitting duty, should the shoe have been on the other foot and Squire was the visitor and Vinny the guide.

He resolved to give his host the benefit of the doubt from here on in.

It proved to be a good decision, as once they reached the roof, the officer in charge could barely be bothered to give Vinny the time of day. Squire dutifully made the rounds of introductions, embellishing the phrase "The International Elite Squad" with a flourish and, occasionally, a mock curtsy as Vinny's face grew as red as the sign above which they stood.

Vinny shook hands with half a dozen high-ranking members of various British law enforcement agencies, none of whom, apparently, had the time of day for the visiting Yank. Having no doubt swooped and scoured every available inch of the rooftop while he'd endured a forced exile of sorts at Squire's favorite pub, the officious and the rank and file alike quickly left Squire and Vinny to their own means. Only the two fresh-faced Bobbies remained at the doorway downstairs, occasionally grinning up at Vinny and Squire between admiring the garishly-painted ladies walking to and fro across the street.

"How's that for bollocks?" Squire spat as he lit one cigarette after the other. Vinny was careful to note that his guide wasn't as sloppy as his appearance might at first imply; each spent butt was quickly extinguished in the palm of Squire's calloused hands and deposited in his left front pants pocket. "We don't even rate an official police escort, just those two pissers standing downstairs with peckers in hand."

"Guess my squad's not so 'elite' after all, eh?" Vinny

asked, feeling himself slipping unconsciously into Squire's guttural street slang.

Squire nodded in the dark, the red haze from the neon sign and his cigarette alternating across his face to give him an almost spectral glow. "Guess they figure you can't do too much damage up here by yourself, Yank. No doubt all the *good* evidence is back at headquarters."

Vinny nodded, reminding himself to put in a quick call to DC and goad his superiors for some kind of trump card he could play tomorrow when he himself visited headquarters to look at the real evidence. For now, though, he sighed and settled in for a long night of collecting what he liked to call "sensual evidence." (The term that earned him no shortage of grief from his old partner, Frank Logan.) It was evidence he couldn't touch, couldn't tag and bag, and sometimes couldn't even *see*. But he could sense it, he could feel it, and it had saved his ass— or solved heretofore unsolvable cases—a dozen or more times in the past.

It was sending him signals now.

"Squire?" he asked as the two shuffled to and from, from one corner of the roof to the other, their feet making crunching noises on the gravel that had broken loose from the coat of tar beneath. "How many sniper cases do you recall getting last year?"

His typically loquacious tour guide was surprisingly succinct. "Nary a one, lad, nary a one."

"And the year before that?" Vinny probed, coming to rest across from the window through which his victim was shot.

"Same," Squire sighed, eager for another pint.

"And before that?"

Squire smiled his big, fat, yellow, crooked toothy grin. "Same, same, and *same*, to answer your next two questions as well as the current. The only way an Englishman knows to shoot another Englishman is face to face. I 'spose it goes back to the old days of dueling, eh? A smack in the face with a glove, two derringers, ten paces, turn and fire and all that. Sniping's not our way, son. We leave that kind of bollocks up to you Yanks."

Vinny moved close to Squire, the dark closing in on them the closer they got to the center of the roof. "But the victim wasn't English, Squire," he fairly whispered. "The victim was a Yank."

Squire tossed the idea off with a shrug. "Makes no nevermind to a Brit. We may be many a thing, but we don't shoot a man from the next roof over. A pub fight here, a torrid love affair there—these might get you a slug on the head with a pint glass or a knife in your gullet, but we're not going to shimmy up the flagpole and plant one dead in your cranium from 100 paces. It's damn undignified, if you ask me."

Vinny nodded, but he wasn't sure if Squire could see his smile in the dark.

7

Frank Logan strolled through the halls of Alex Ritchey's dorm building and felt old enough to be gripping the sides of a stainless steel walker, complete with tennis balls on each leg to muffle the noise, and wearing a pair of Depends.

Rock music blared from each room he passed—he supposed you would call it "rock," though it sure didn't sound like the Hendrix and Stones he grew up on—and glimpses inside spoke of opium dens or brothels, not the storied halls of academia the private school's brochure would lead you to believe.

Posters of pot leaves and alternative bands he'd never heard of before lined the walls as boys and girls—he had yet to get used to calling them young men and women—strutted around in various stages of undress, as confident in their exposed stomachs and shoulders as they were in their uncertain futures.

In a surreal contrast to the party atmosphere down the hall, stark yellow crime scene tape still fluttered around the doorway of Alex's room. A campus security guard sat on a folding chair in the corner facing the room, resting his feet on a water fountain and devouring the latest issue of *Extreme Fighting Digest*. Even though the man was sitting, Frank could see he had a hulking figure, and it was equally clear he was no stranger to a broken nose or bar fight.

After assuring himself that Alex's old roommate and latest girlfriend were both seated quietly inside the room, as he'd requested of them earlier in the day, he flashed his PI badge at the rent-a-cop. "Evening, officer," he said with forced enthusiasm, although it was hard not to bite his tongue off in the process. "Name's Frank Logan. I'm here on official business concerning young Mr. Ritchey. That's his room there and...."

"I know why you're here, Pops," the guard said, glaring at Frank, his eyes as crooked and bent as his flat, fleshy nose. "Sniffing around for the kid's old man. I read all about it in this morning's paper." The guard nudged a stack of reading material on the floor with his foot. "My supervisor told me to let you have ten minutes with each kid, tops. One minute, scratch that, one *second* over and I'm escorting your grizzled ass off campus. Got me?"

Frank eyed the man with a practiced grin, cocking his head to one side in a practiced response that worked to buy him some precious time to control his already overheating emotions. Ah, what a little bit of power could do for an even smaller man. "Yes, *sir*," Frank replied sardonically, resisting the urge to salute as he tried the honey versus vinegar approach. "I was hoping for fifteen minutes, though. Anyway I could convince you to...."

"No can do, Pops," the guard said with a grin, enjoying himself. "And every minute you spend out here trying to convince me is another minute I deduct from your twenty. You're already down to 19, old man. Care to go for 18?"

"Heavens no," Frank replied. "I don't want you to waste another brain cell counting that high. It's clear you're running on empty as it is. Good day, sir."

By the time the guard realized he'd been insulted, Frank had slipped into Alex's dorm room, slammed the door shut, locked it, and barred the passage with a desk chair. The two dorm rats leapt to their feet at Frank's appearance, but he settled them quickly with a warm smile and a quick flash of his oversized PI badge, even as the guard began banging on the door.

"Don't mind him." Frank smiled as he lifted his overcoat to sit on the corner of Alex's desk. "Apparently he's just discovered the use of his opposable thumbs."

The kids chuckled politely, then looked back down at their feet. Normally, Frank would have preferred to interview them both separately, but it had taken him a week just to get access to both of them at once, let alone on their own. He feared this was his one and only shot, and damned if he wasn't going to make good use of it, all 18 minutes he had remaining.

He was trying hard not to let the reversal of fortune affect his detecting skills. Having limited access to files, detectives, witnesses, and evidence was a real shock to him, and he was hard-pressed to come up with better alternatives than the old tried and true. Still, he'd known it was coming; now he just had to deal with it.

"Dominic Pasquale?" he asked, addressing the pasty Goth kid sitting on the bed next to Mandy Sullivan. The kid looked up through a swatch of ink-black hair and nodded politely. "I know we don't have a lot of time here." Frank's eyes shifted to the front door for emphasis. "I'll cut right to the chase. Do you know anybody, anybody at all, who might want to hurt Alex?"

Dominic shook his head, but volunteered nothing verbal. Frank knew the type; polite but rebellious. The kid obviously trusted authority about as much as he trusted his appeal to the opposite sex, which, judging from the nauseated look on Mandy's face, was less than nil.

"He hadn't had any run-ins with his professors?" Frank prodded, gently but insistently. "Didn't cut anybody off in traffic? Hadn't stolen anybody's table in the cafeteria?"

Dominic gave a quick but firm nod to each of Frank's questions. "How about *you*?" he asked pointedly, switching gears abruptly to try to stump the kid. "You two come from pretty different worlds, huh? Alex has the cash, the car, the right classes, the girl, the clothes…that didn't irk you just a little? Your relationship wasn't strained at all?"

The kid smiled for the first time since Frank entered the room. "Yeah, I watch *The Closer* too, you know. This reverse psychology shit ain't gonna work on me. I saw Alex's world, but I didn't envy it. Mandy? She's cool, but not my type, you know. Nothing personal, Mandy."

He looked at her from under his black mop to make sure he hadn't given offense and, when she smiled reassuringly at him to continue, he did. "I'm not going to lie. Alex and I were never gonna be the kind of college roommates who went into business after school or started our own IPO or ran each other's political campaigns, you know? It wasn't going to be like that.

"But we weren't enemies or anything, either. Alex, well, he wasn't like the other prepsters who go here. He looked the part, but he didn't *play* the part, you know? There was more to him than that. I'd be reading a book and he'd come in and ask me what it was about. I'd lend it to him when I was through and he'd actually read it. I even burned him a few of my CDs, thinking no way would he dig them but, a few days later, I'd hear them playing in his car or something as he drove by on campus. He was just a good guy; nothing more, nothing less. I don't know who would want to hurt him. Honest."

For some reason Frank believed him, and nodded somberly to reveal as much. "Did you two talk much? Share any deep dark secrets that might help me out?"

Dominic snorted. "Like what? Did I tell him why I ended up this way? No, not likely. It wasn't like that. We kept it on the surface; I think Alex was deeper than he let on, though. He didn't go deep when we talked. It was movies and classes and girls and stuff, but I sensed he was…deeper.

"He asked a lot about me, about other people, but when you tried to return the favor, he'd clam up. Not so a casual observer would notice, but he'd answer, like, one insignificant thing you'd asked and deflect the conversation right back to you. It was subtle, but I noticed him doing it more and more often as the semester continued and we got to know each other a little better."

Frank nodded. Leisurely, almost casually, he let his eyes bore into Dominic's, hoping to see a blush cross his cheeks or a drop of sweat roll down his forehead, but the kid was solid. There was nothing there. He next let his gaze fall on Mandy, who was not quite so cool.

"Same here," she snapped, perhaps a little more quickly—not to mention harshly—than she'd intended. "I mean, don't even bother asking. He didn't open up to me any more than he did with Dominic here."

"I doubt that," Frank smiled, oozing forgiveness. "You mean there was no pillow talk, no candlelit confessions over a bottle or two of wine from his father's private vineyard? I find that a little hard to believe."

Mandy blushed, but Frank had the feeling it was more from memory than guilt. "Not like you're thinking, sir. I mean, okay, you could tell he didn't care that much for his dad, but it wasn't a running theme or anything. I'm the same way about my mom. We've all got baggage with our folks, right? Big deal, right? Right?"

Frank nodded as the tone of Mandy's voice rose. She was clearly a pretty girl, but her façade had gradually begun to fray at the edges in the wake of her boyfriend's disappearance. She looked farm-fed and well-bred, a pretty, perky, ripe peach with good intentions and a better body.

He smiled approvingly at her, hoping it might calm her nerves. It didn't. Frank let the two adolescents cool their heels for a second. The silence in the room made the banging at the door that much more deafening. Still, the two sat patiently, eyeing the floor instead of each other.

Frank admired the room, noting that only Alex's possessions still remained. "Dominic?" he asked, hanging a thumb toward the blank walls and empty bunk on his side of the room.

"School policy," the kid admitted sheepishly, as if he'd had anything to do with it. "I've been moved until the end of the semester, whether Alex comes back…or not. If he doesn't, I get an automatic 'A' for the term."

Both Frank and Dominic shot a glance at Mandy in the wake of his confession. The two kids looked at each other, one apologizing, one forgiving, until both finally returned their attention back to Frank.

"Me too," Mandy admitted, almost guiltily. "School policy."

Frank nodded. It was hardly motivation for the crime of the century, particularly since he'd checked the transcripts of both kids and they were straight-A's, all the way. Almost apologetically—the private sector must have softened him—he asked Mandy and Dominic to stand on the empty side of the room, and began meticulously going through Alex's things. It didn't take long; there wasn't much left. Some beer girl posters, a few bootleg CDs, a smut mag or two, his lacrosse stick, a hamper full of dirty laundry—pretty typical dorm rat stuff, as far as Frank was concerned. Apparently, the local detectives had taken what the family had deemed "unimportant," leaving Frank with some half-finished research papers and a few back issues of *Entrepreneur* magazine. Clearly, Alex was being groomed for the fast track.

Frank was trying to decipher the hieroglyphics on some art film movie poster, his hand leaning on Alex's desk, when a small voice from behind him said, almost apologetically, "His dad already took it."

Expecting Mandy to be the source of the confession, he was surprised to find that Dominic had crept up behind him, perhaps none too eager for Mandy to hear what they were saying. Taking a cue from the kid, Frank leaned in close and asked, "Took *what*, Dominic?"

"The diary," the kid said, his face finally coming to life as a rosy blush filled his fine, almost delicate features. "The one Alex wrote in every night. Isn't that what you're looking for?"

"It wasn't," Frank admitted, already striding for the door and leaving the two freshmen, pale-faced, in his wake. "But I sure am now."

The security guard stumbled into the room the minute Frank moved the chair that had been wedged against the knob. His presence filled the tiny room, and Frank almost smiled to note Dominic and Mandy clutching each other in their barren corner.

"Hey, asshole," the guard said, already up and at 'em as he squared off in front of Frank. "I could have your license for that, you know."

Frank had no intention of fighting the steroid beast, and quickly pulled his overcoat back to reveal the holster resting firmly against his hip. Though the gun was not loaded, both its girth and its glint were impressive enough to halt the rent-a-cop in his tracks.

Reaching for his own belt, the guard came back with

something big, black, and shiny, surprising them both: it was a walkie-talkie. From behind him, Dominic and Mandy broke into nervous laughter, most likely their first since Alex disappeared.

As he strode away from the abbreviated confrontation, Frank muttered a muted chuckle to himself.

8

The Sniper was already back at work. He sat in the roughhewn Mexican bar, nursing his third *cerveza* of the morning. It felt smooth and crisp on his tongue, and it bothered him little to be drinking so early in the day. His jet lag was still in permanent hangover mode, so as far as he was concerned, a few ice cold Dos Equis and some stale tortillas were little more than hair of the dog.

Besides, he'd never been one of those regimented, calculated professionals you see on TV or the movies. He was expertly trained, at the top of his game, some might say, but more important to his profession, he'd been doubly blessed by his age and proclivities. In other words, he was young and a crack shot. It was that simple. Five years from now, he might not be able to get the job done. Of course, by then, it would already be over.

Ever on the alert, his eyes scanned the bar in a perpetual side-to-side motion. His field of vision was enhanced thanks to his careful choice of tables, and the mid-morning sun camouflaged his constant eye movements as sunlight filtered through the holes in the rusty tin roof and barged in through the open air courtyard.

Loud Motley Crue music played on a ratty old jukebox in the corner as a trio of locals hunkered at the bar scoped him out. The Sniper tapped his fingers on the splintered table, toying with his discarded lime and several tortilla crumbs as he whiled away the morning, waiting for his latest target to come into focus.

He enjoyed retro music. He enjoyed most things. He was, after all, a sensual animal. He liked life, period. It didn't matter what was happening, or where he was, or what he was doing, he enjoyed himself. In that, he was something of a dichotomy: a killer who enjoyed life, even as he was dealing out death.

His tastes were eclectic, varied, and many. Sunsets, candles, a cold beer, loud music, classical music, young girls, older women. Books, magazines, the Internet, hotels, room service, fine wine, generic soda, a snub-nosed pistol or a sawed-off shotgun.

He was no death snob, that was for sure. There was no favorite gun or nicknamed weapon. Indeed, he always traveled empty-handed. No luggage, no contacts, no cell phone or laptop or ball cap or favorite T-shirt. He was alone, incognito, an inconspicuous young man flying solo, quickly able to get lost in the crowd and slip, unnoticed, through airport security.

If he wore a cheap backpack, it was simply because he knew passengers without any carry-on luggage aroused suspicion, but inside was little more than a fresh paperback from the airport gift shop, some aspirin, and a few Slim Jims or Skittles in case he got hungry on the flight.

Even his wallet held the bare minimum; a phony ID, some VISA gift cards in increments of $100, a wad of American Express traveler's checks, some movie stubs of the latest Hollywood blockbusters. No more, no less. He enjoyed it that way.

He had no ties, no permanent address, no safe house or phone number or potted plant. There was the smattering of bank accounts, anonymous and untraceable, for the most part, from which he acquired his funds and received payment, but those were, quite literally, his only ties to the material world.

He had no future; that much was clear. In his line of work, no matter how good you were, there was always some slip-up, some flub, some miscalculation that led to a quick capture and a slow demise.

Barring detection and capture by the authorities, there was also the unscrupulous client who would rather kill you than pay your fee, or the upstart young rival who figured the best way to make his bones quickly—and skip paying his dues altogether—was to off the best and the brightest, killing two birds with one stone.

Even the best went down, so why fight it?

He was far from sloppy, but he knew others that were downright anal about avoiding detection, shaving their bodies and wearing elaborate body suits to eliminate trace evidence, blowing up entire buildings to assure no one would ever discover a single bullet casing.

What the fuck? He was no angel, far from it, but the day he killed a building full of innocent people just to save his own ass, he was no longer a professional assassin, but instead a sad, miserable, selfish asshole who just happened to kill people for a living.

Where, he wondered, was the joy in *that*?

The Sniper smiled, and signaled the barmaid for another *cerveza*. She nodded, but he was quick to notice that the wiliest of the trio at the bar—he'd avoided thinking of them as the "Three Amigos" so far, even though the term was dutifully appropriate—slid over some local coins and offered to bring it over for her.

She held up her hands quizzically, and the Sniper nodded without hesitation. Although he had no weapon, there was no fear in his heart. He knew he looked like the typical American tourist, on vacation, taking a break from his studies, on a summer work relief mission, whatever. He could pass for most ages within a range of ten to twenty years, and when he was in southern climes, as he was today, he preferred the Old Navy look: cargo pants, fake pizza delivery T-shirt, flip-slops, a three-day beard, cheap sunglasses, frayed ball cap, the ever-present camouflage backpack.

No wonder they'd been eyeing him all morning. The Good Samaritan arrived with the cold beer in his chapped, leathery hands, the condensation beating a crooked path down his abbreviated lifeline. He put it down on the table and then sat down across from the Sniper. His smile was bright but icy, wide but pinched. To the trained eye, his intentions couldn't be more obvious.

"I am Diego," he said in smooth, satiny English. There was the trace of an accent, but it was clear Diego was as familiar with life across the border as he was in his own country. "Nice to meet you."

"Have we met?" the Sniper asked icily, his harsh expression in direct contrast to his open, casual attire; it was like hearing a cat bark. "You've introduced yourself, but I'm afraid I won't be returning the favor."

Diego smiled warmly nonetheless. "Understood. No pleasure, just business, eh?" When the Sniper merely regarded his new beer, Diego propositioned him: "Care for a good time this morning, sir? My little sister's out back. Just turned sixteen." Diego flashed a winning smile, leaning back from the bar to reveal bronze skin and six-pack abs pressing against his dirty, tight tank top. "She's almost as pretty as I am."

The Sniper said nothing, sipped his beer, and finally shook his head.

Diego smiled in reply, and then placed an old pistol against the Sniper's knee. "Like I said, she's very, *very* pretty. Worth every penny you have in your wallet, eh?"

The Sniper noticed that the colder Diego's eyes grew, the stronger his accent became. By now, he sounded reminiscent of Tony Montana in *Scarface*. He also knew there was no way out of the barter. There was no prepubescent sister waiting outside for him, panting and wet, only the cold hard steel of an old gun pressed against the vulnerable flesh of his white, American knee.

This was Mexico, a lawless land of robbers and barons. He was sitting across from a robber. That was all there was to it. Politically incorrect? Perhaps, but at the moment neither politics nor correctness had anything to do with it. This was life or death, cultural sensitivities be damned. Flashing a sideways glance at the other two amigos, the Sniper saw them patting their waistbands. More guns.

Great.

The Sniper smiled. "Sounds fun," he said. "I just hope your sister's as good a lay as your mamacita, Diego. I suppose by now I'm ready to go again."

Diego's face grew ashen as the Sniper stood up abruptly. His two friends rose, and together the four left the restaurant through a side entrance. On the way out, he made sure to grab his beer. The Sniper let two of the locals amble in front of him, noticing the third kept watch in the back. Diego led the way, past the kitchen, toward a back entrance featuring a tiny patio with two tables and an outdoor clay fireplace for those cool Mexican evenings.

Little jalapeno porch lights were strung in a haphazard square around a dilapidated fence that kept the patio separate, if only barely, from the used tire shop-slash-garage next door.

Even now the Sniper could hear the whirr-whirr of an outdated lug-nut gun and the swish-whoosh of bald tires hitting the dusty Mexican clay of an unpaved garage floor.

Two in front. One behind. Three guns. Lucky he'd slept last night. Maybe his jet lag wasn't so bad after all. The sun was high as he smashed his beer bottle against the first steel patio table he passed. Beer splashed cold and fresh against the tops of his bare feet as he whirled on his flip-flops to insert the jagged bottle edge into the throat of the man directly behind him. It was met with little resistance, and he even had time to spin around before a torrent of thick, red arterial blood sprayed from the man's open—and quite lethal—wound. It passed by his ear with an audible hiss, and as he watched the splatter splash the dry brick wall out of the corner of his eye, he was reminded vaguely of a water ride he'd ridden at some theme park or another.

Typical protocol would have been to eliminate the two men in front of him first, but the man behind him was bigger, and already had his gun out. He had felt it in the small of his back as they passed the threshold from restaurant to patio.

Besides, now he had the time to turn and meet the two men in front. He dispatched the second stranger first, kneeling to sever the femoral artery in his thigh and thus disorienting Diego as he instinctively aimed his gun at chest height.

As the Sniper rose, he inserted the bloody, dulled bottle edge just under and to the left of Diego's ribcage, severing numerous internal organs but not inflicting an immediately lethal blow. He wanted the third death to last.

As Diego's gun clattered to the dirty tile floor, the Sniper reached to pick it up. He checked the chamber to see five bullets, all in passable shape, the gun itself ancient but more than effective. He would have to try it out first before he carried out his mission, of course, but that would still leave him four bullets. It would have to be a close-up job, but he'd save a few grand on the high-powered rifle he was supposed to score from a local arms dealer later that afternoon.

Sweet! Quickly, he dragged the two unnamed men into the corner, covering them with a tarp used to cover the woodpile next to the fireplace. It wouldn't hide the bodies for long, and no doubt the barmaid was in cahoots and would find them shortly after the Sniper left, but what did he care? His mission would soon be over, and by the time the Federales caught up to him, he'd be long gone.

Lastly he turned to Diego, watching as his bronze skin turned a pasty caramel, then sallow yellow, and finally pale vanilla. The light left his eyes gradually as his blood filled the dusty grout of a long-neglected floor. His mouth said nothing as he died, though his desperate, pleading, panic-stricken eyes spoke volumes. The Sniper took no joy in the death, but neither did he let himself feel remorse.

Would Diego and his men have killed him? Probably not. Most likely they would have robbed him, beat him, threatened him, and sent him back to the bar with fingers over their lips and smiles on their faces, a cocky swagger in their walk and pockets full of crumpled American bills. Another gringo tourist fallen prey to the local hooligans.

Were his actions justified? Had the killings been necessary? Was his conscience free of guilt? Who cared? He had a job to do and they were in his way, Diego and his thugs. Simple as that. Sweat dripped in the Sniper's eyes and he blinked himself back to reality.

The life had left Diego's eyes now; the Sniper pressed them closed and kissed his forehead tenderly, almost gingerly, respectfully. He wiped the moisture from his face, glancing up at the bright morning sun. By noon the blood would be dry, blending into the gay ceramic pattern of the patio floor. Maybe he had longer than he thought.

After Diego's death he dragged him to the tarp by the woodpile, where he joined his friends. The Sniper said a quick prayer, crossed himself, and then returned to the sleepy Mexican restaurant, gun down his pants, blood-flecked fingers raised to signal the quizzical barmaid he needed another beer.

In all the hubbub, he almost missed seeing his mark walk into the bar. *Almost*.

Arnold "Arnie" Kinsey loved Mexico. Always had; always would. Which was a good thing, considering he might be living there for quite some time or, at least, until this latest mess died down. When his business partners suggested they should all split up and head for the four corners of the earth "for a while," Arnie figured, *Why go halfway around the world just to avoid extradition? Why not Mexico?*

So here he was, settled in a sweet cabana down by the ocean and enjoying *cervezas* with lunch and pitchers of margaritas with dinner. Though his partners warned against it, he ambled into town at least once a day, typically in the morning, picking up a fresh order of enchiladas from his new favorite bar and sipping a cold Tecate—his first of the day—while he waited.

Arnie had just turned a venerable 60 years old, and his pasty white skin had since turned a leathery brown from his near week of basking in the Mexican sun. He didn't feel 60 anymore, not since leaving the daily grind of his work back in the States, anyway. He felt positively alive, hell, practically... *vibrant*! (Not a word he would have used to describe himself as little as seven short days ago!) How wonderful to not be tied down by the constant stream of memos, messages, emails, faxes, phone calls, and meetings of corporate life.

The Mexicans really had the right idea; work hard, but work slow. Embrace life; enjoy it. Work with your hands, love the earth, cherish it, and be rewarded with a style of life few Americans could ever enjoy. If only they'd let themselves....

He felt the sunlight on his shoulders and wondered how long it had been since he'd felt like this back home. He'd been on vacations before, sure, but this...this was something different. He rarely saw the sun in his former life, arriving at the office long before sunup and getting home long after sunset. The light he did see all day came from miles and miles of overhead tubing, or the occasional glance out his corner office window to the Washington Monument in the distant foreground.

To think he'd been missing this, all of this, and never even realizing it. It made his head swim, and the Tecate only helped reinforce his feeling of separation from his current life. With every sip, it seemed, he became less the man he was and more the man he wanted to be.

As he walked that morning, getting used to his new sandals and still picking the sand out of his ass from his early morning swim, he shifted his Hawaiian shirt—one of six different designs he'd picked up in the hotel gift shop—until it felt more comfortable over his potbelly. The sun felt warm on his sunburned pate and he shuffled slowly, his leather sandals kicking up tufts of clay-filled dust from the packed dirt streets of this little Mexican resort town he'd selected for his self-imposed exile.

Arnie was formulating a plan, one his business partners didn't know about or, if they had, would hardly approve of. He had enough offshore accounts to live this way—suntanned, Hawaiian-shirted, beer buzzed, saltwater-logged—for the rest of his natural life. He planned to do so.

In fact, he already *was* doing so.

The officials at the local bank—half of them in Hawaiian shirts and sandals as well—had been more than eager to set up a local account in his name, or at least the name he was going by here, thanks to some nifty forged documents a la another local businessman: Roger Robertson. (Awkward, yes, but he had a bad memory and this way he could remember his forced identity easier. It was also a little less obvious than the preferred John Smith.)

Day by day, he siphoned a little more from Switzerland and Austria and elsewhere around the globe to Mexico, where the sun shone, the azure waters glistened, the beer was cold and the margaritas salty.

He was ordering his first cold beer of the day, savoring its first tingly sip, when the young man from the patio walked in. Arnie nodded in his direction, but the man seemed…distracted. It wasn't entirely strange to see another American south of the border, but strange enough to warrant a smile in passing or, barring that, at least a conspiratorial nod.

Oh well, maybe Arnie would see him at the hotel restaurant later that night and they could catch up on all the news from the States then. After all, it was the best restaurant in town. Looking at the back of the young man's head as he sat down at a table alone and sipped at a fresh beer, he wondered if maybe he'd seen him there once or twice before.

He looked oddly familiar.

10

Vinny waited with Squire outside of the outdated conference room in the neighborhood precinct that was doubling for the "Piccadilly Pick-off" headquarters. Like "The Maze Murders" before it and a dozen lively nicknames after it, Vinny was never shocked to hear how callously murder was given an identity by the local press. (You had to give those Brits credit, though; their newspaper headlines were a lot more colorful than back in the States.)

The "sniper shot heard round the world," as the local paper's inglorious subheading read, was better known to the newspaper's readers than it was to the town's constables, who had little to go on since the American's murder two days hence. To date no one had determined the man's identity, the motive for his death, nor even the time of death, for that matter. To Vinny, a man used to having a thousand different resources at his fingers any time of day or night, the mystery was only half as annoying as the bloody red tape.

The bullet fragments, gunpowder residue, and physical evidence that Vinny would have had days ago as a federal agent were as yet unknown to him. Thanks to his inexperience with working with foreign officers of the law, or any hint of help from the brass back home, he had no idea *when* they would be known to him, if ever. His foreign hosts might have spoken the same language, but Vinny felt like he needed a translator just to get his point across.

Now Vinny tapped his foot nervously and held the FBI stationary in his hand, bearing a fresh fax from his superiors requesting—frankly, just short of *demanding*—the local law enforcement to let him view the files on the deceased American businessman "forthwith."

Never one to step out of character, Squire smoked non-stop as Vinny begrudgingly became used to the ever-present halo of nicotine and ashes that now followed them like the cloud of dirt surrounding that Pig Pen character in the *Peanuts* holiday specials he'd always loved so much as a kid.

Smoke or no smoke, Vinny had to hand it to his new pal Squire. He'd been more than a liaison, babysitter or ambassador over the past 48 hours; he'd been downright congenial, having dinner with Vinny in his budget hotel room (fish and chips, natch), and coming to the door with a six-pack of his beloved Guinness and a tin of the shortbread cookies Vinny had become so fond of. They ate most meals together, in fact, and it was Squire who had snuck him back into the crime scenes on two separate occasions.

Both had been less than helpful.

As the two men suffered in silence, save for the incessant crackling of Squire's endless cigarette paper and occasional coughing, Vinny wallowed in self-pity, failure, and professional embarrassment. At first, he'd been flattered by Flaherty's promotion. The International Elite Squad. It sounded so good at first blush, the ten-dollar words fairly rolling off one's tongue, but now Vinny realized he was neither international or, for that matter, *elite*. So far he'd managed to impress not a single local. (Even Squire looked at him with something less like respect and more like endurance.)

For once Vinny's charming smile, his dashing looks, his physical aptitude, even his locker room humor and put-on

Sopranos airs had gotten him nowhere with the stolid, stodgy, and stubborn local detectives, an experience as new to him as it was humbling.

Vinny had come up against resistance from locals before. During his time with senior partner Frank Logan on the now-infamous Maze Murders—later chronicled in a bestselling true crime book by the same name, with his partner as the author—Vinny had had his fair share of run-ins with the various towns in which the sadistic serial killer known as "Maze" had struck.

During that case, however, Vinny had flourished. He might have started out as a rookie, but after a few days with Frank he'd known just when to use muscle and just when to use a smile. His "vinegar or honey" meter, as Frank had always called it, worked quite well. Perhaps he'd gotten spoiled. On foreign soil, at least so far, *nothing* was working.

Now Vinny knew that he would get nowhere without the police file, and the British brass were still dragging their feet. Vinny was due to fly back to DC later that afternoon, empty-handed, it would seem, and he and Squire had been cooling their heels all morning, waiting for some kind of decision from the higher-ups. The fax in Vinny's hand, from none other than Senior Director Flaherty himself, was all but useless. It had been cc'd to the very men holding up the process.

Squire chortled, snuffing out another cigarette on the heel of his shoe before burying it in the overflowing ashbin at his feet. "Looks like you're getting the famous British treatment, mate," he sighed before elaborating: "cold and ugly."

Vinny snorted back. He was too irate to talk. "This is barbaric," he finally spat. "How can I solve the crime if I can't get a look at the file? I don't even know who the victim is yet."

Squire nodded. "Listen, maybe if you weren't working for

a squad called the 'International Elite,' you might not face so many closed doors. Humble's the way to play it, that's my take."

"Squire, I've been humble. I've been gracious. I've even been kind, for chrissakes. Now I'm going to rip the door off the hinges and find out what I need to know."

Vinny stood up, but Squire held him back with a gentle but firm grip. "Not now, mate. You're very, very close."

When Vinny sat back down, Squire lit up another cigarette, inhaled in an achingly slow fashion, and then pointed to the board room, outside which they'd been holding vigil since first light. "What's going on in there, mate, is a famous bit of foreign freeze-out. You'll get a look at the files, trust me. You'll find out who your man is, you bet. But first they want to make sure *we* look our best. You know, was it our fault that sniper got on the Coke roof. Was it a local? Or one of your own? That type of stuff, you know. 'Fess up, you'd do the same if the shoe was on the other foot, right?"

Vinny nodded, sighed, and almost reached for Squire's cigarette. He nodded again, as if convincing himself, until at last—with two hours to go before Squire was due to drive him back to Heathrow—the door to the conference room finally opened up and half a dozen glum-looking local dicks walked out with a decidedly un-British swagger.

"All yours, mate," they coughed in unison, turning the corner; their snickers followed them down the hall.

Vinny couldn't have cared less; he was up off the old wooden bench and in the conference room before Squire had a chance to extinguish his smoke, let alone stand up and follow.

He could have waited; inside the cavernous room, on a polished wooden table that looked as if it had been borrowed from some old baron or duke, sat a single manila file folder, pristine and untattered, bearing a single typed sheet of paper.

It read, simply:

```
Name: Philip Bronstein
Race: Caucasian
Sex: Male
Age: 62
DOB: 8/12/1943
Weight: 237
Residence: American citizen
Employment: CEO, SouthCom Digital, LLC
Cause of death: severe trauma to head
Device of death: high-caliber bullet
Bullet fragments: being processed/TBD
```

That was it. 10 lines on an otherwise blank page, and the only two things of value were the man's name and place of employment. Vinny fumed silently. He had less than an hour at the precinct, and who knew when the evidence would be "processed." A strange calm came over him. He put his hand on Squire's shoulder and whispered, "Take me home, mate."

Squire saluted him properly, and together they walked out.

11

Frank Logan sat in his office, bristling at the slow pace of his (in his mind anyway) overly-priced computer. It wasn't that he was cheap; not exactly. It was just that he'd gotten spoiled working on a federal budget, where no matter what he asked for or how much it cost, he usually got it.

Say what you want about the Feds, he mused silently to himself as he waited for yet another webpage to load on his super-size-me flat computer monitor, *but their computers kicked ass on this thing.*

"Dana!" he cried out for perhaps the sixth time in a minute. "Something's wrong with this computer again."

Even over the smooth jazz floating in from the reception area, he heard Dana chuckle as she rose from her chair to amble in on her long, coltish legs, made doubly so by the wobbly heels on which she teetered. He eyed her coolly over the top of his monitor; she was in her casual Friday garb—although it was only Thursday—which meant a daringly short skirt and shimmering black halter top that came dangerously close to exposing her flat, fit midriff.

Her skin was Indian summer tan, her nails short and bitten to the quick, her nose slightly crooked, adding character, not comedy, to an appealing face that was open, fresh and, most tantalizingly of all, young. She might have looked like the quintessential mid-life secretarial hire, but Frank was well past his midlife crisis and, to sound cliché, much more interested in the enthusiasm and vitality of her mind, not the firmness of her skin or supple way her throat blended into her high, small breasts.

The best part was, Dana was stolidly unavailable. She'd made that quite clear when she'd interviewed for the job, the two of them sitting across from each other on the newly-delivered reception office furniture, her business suit tight but subdued, her resume impressive and presented in a new leather portfolio.

"I'm engaged," she'd said matter-of-factly when he asked about her personal life. He'd been looking for her to rattle off her hobbies, her favorite book, a sport or two like all the other gals had answered. When he stared pointedly at her bare, if tan, ring finger, she'd added, somewhat defensively, "he's still in school and we can't afford a ring. He's a writer; like you, Mr. Logan. I thought, hiring on, I could learn the tools of the trade and maybe pick up some writing tips along the way."

"Not to mention pay the bills so you're starving writer doesn't starve," Frank had added, making her smile. Her answer—not to mention her marital status or fiance's occupation—had mattered little; he'd decided to hire her the minute she'd walked through the door. She had a slightly Italian air, reminding him of his old partner Vinny, whom he missed more than he expected, and an authoritarian bearing that reminded him of his old receptionist, Margie, who had worked with him for nearly three decades. The combination, he had to admit, was as unexpected as it was comforting.

He didn't care about her qualifications, her freshly minted diploma, her GPA, her night school classes in Criminology, her pedigree. He just needed someone to answer the phones and help him with the damn computer.

She was earning her money today.

"There's nothing wrong with your computer, Frank," she said with a smile, whispering across the carpet and gliding to the side of his desk. They'd long since given up the formality of "Mr. Logan" and he'd been glad to hear that she'd never once called him *sir*. "You're just too cheap to spring for DSL, so instead you bought a second line for dial-up and, nothing personal, but dial-up sucks."

They shared a father-daughter thing he was beginning to enjoy a little too much for his liking. He was the doddering old fool to her plucky, sassy coed, never bristling when she called him cheap or old-fashioned or a gentleman. In fact, he kind of liked it. Over the years there had been a wife, an affair, a divorce, and no kids.

In the obsession that was his career, he'd never looked back, never thought twice about regret or love or companionship or fatherhood. Now his days were full of empty hours and little errands; a background check here, grocery shopping on the way home, picking out a DVD at the local Blockbuster every other night.

He was growing suburban, and though he didn't mind the leisure time or the scent of aromatherapy candles that filled his quiet hours or the smooth jazz that set the tone at work, he missed the companionship of his comrades in arms, missed his old Gal Friday Margie and her wise-cracking airs and little holiday gift baskets.

Dana seemed to fill that void, if not expertly, then at least promptly. Yes, she was beautiful, a "comely lass," as his old boss Flaherty would have called her, tight and fit and taut and ripe, but the quick double-takes he threw at her high ass or long legs, the waft of her perfume as she bustled into the room with this form or that for him to sign, the heft of her breasts as she bent over to point out where he'd forgotten to initial something, were purely physical reactions. Nothing more, nothing less.

What drove him to get to work early to greet her, what led him to find things for her to do later and later each evening before she left him to a lonely night of New Releases from Blockbuster and the latest aromatherapy scent in his empty living room was her vitality, her humor, her gift of being there when he needed her, and that foxhole feeling that two people formed when working together in the same 800-square foot office five days a week, 8 or 9 hours per day.

Even now, as she fiddled with his computer settings and double-clicked his little trash can icon to free up some hard-drive space, he drank in her presence like a solar panel sucks up the sun. What's worse, she knew it.

"Look, Frank," she sighed good-naturedly, standing up after doing her best to speed up his web surfing, "you could do all this yourself. I know, you're my boss, right? I got it, but I'm pretty sure you couldn't run the FBI or whatever you did and write, like, ten gabillion books and not know your way around Yahoo or Google, you know what I mean?"

Then he did something that surprised even himself: He giggled. No, it was more of a twitter. He couldn't help it; it just came out. *God*, he thought, *what an ass I've become!*

"Sit down a minute," he said grimly, perhaps overcompensating for the twitter or giggle or chortle or whatever had escaped his lungs before his mouth had a chance to shut it down. She sighed, smoothed out the back of her skirt, sat down in the pricey leather chair across from his desk, and crossed her legs primly. "Please don't give me another lecture about my car, Frank. It's fine. Nothing an oil change or tune-up wouldn't fix, all...."

Frank smiled and shook his head. He *had* been getting on her lately about that little import she drove. It sputtered and coughed, fouled up the parking lot with numerous oil leaks and constantly made her late to work. Not that there was a line of clients waiting at the door, but *he'd* been waiting.

He didn't like waiting.

"No, Dana, it's not the car. It's about our client."

Her eyes perked up. She loved to talk shop. He realized suddenly he should do that more with her. Involve her. Include her. He decided to make up for lost time and asked her, quite seriously, as if she were an expert consultant and not his new Gal Friday, "What do you know about Arthur Ritchey?"

"You mean besides the fact that he's a gazillionaire? Besides the half a dozen companies he owns and his yacht and his gorgeous wife…?"

"Dana?" he cut her off. "I can read *Time* magazine as well as you can. What I mean is, what do you know about him from what you've seen personally? Here? In the office? When he comes to rattle my cage or check on my progress?"

She smiled. "What's this, Frank? My birthday or something? You're asking *me* my opinion? On a case?"

"Yes, Dana, your opinion. On a case. What do you think Mr. Ritchey's true intentions are?"

"You mean, besides finding his son? Well, I'll tell you, my senior year at Georgetown I had the opportunity to clerk for either a local law firm or a local private investigator. I knew the law firm would look better on my resume, but I chose the PI. I guess that's just me. Don't roll your eyes, I'm getting to the point here, which is just this: Clients would come into the office twice. Once to tell my boss their problem. Their husband was cheating, their wife was opening offshore accounts in Switzerland or wherever. Their boyfriends were gay, whatever. Then they'd let my boss do his job. The second, and last, time they'd come in was when he showed them that either what they suspected was true or they were full of it, you know? He'd throw some pictures down on the table in a plain brown wrapper or some photocopies of hidden assets or a hidden video of the babysitter slapping the kids, whatever. That was it.

"They didn't make a big show out of stopping by every week, bringing me flavored coffees or putting on airs, asking about my day. They barely looked at me. They didn't want to be there, my old boss's clients. They'd shuffle in, wait across from my desk with their head down, staring at their shoes, and the minute he was done with them, they couldn't wait to leave. Maybe this guy Ritchey's just a showboat. Maybe he's just used to having an audience, I dunno, but I'm just telling you the difference between most clients and *this* guy."

Frank nodded solemnly, as if delivering a verdict. "Yeah," he said finally. "I think he's dirty, too."

"You do?" she asked conspiratorially, subconsciously leaning forward in her seat and uncrossing her legs. "Why?"

He nodded again, trying not to notice. "Two reasons. First, you don't wait a week to hire a private investigator. Second, you don't lie about missing evidence."

"*What* missing evidence?" By now she was practically sitting on top of his desk.

"When I went to visit the kid's dorm room yesterday, the roommate told me Alex had kept a diary. Now, I don't think there are any clues in it. I don't think it's our smoking gun, but I do think his father not telling me he has it makes him dirty."

She nodded, her face serious and attentive, not to mention six inches closer to his than when she had first sat down. He liked that. "Listen," he sighed, "I don't want you getting the wrong idea, Dana, but I need a partner on this. I need someone smart, someone savvy, someone young, someone new, someone, more importantly, without my face, to go snooping around

Ritchey's background. I know his companies, know his finances, but I need to know him personally. In my experience, I've found women to be the best partners on this kind of job. Start with the wife. Find out what you can. Then look deeper. Find out if Ritchey's had affairs, given lavish gifts to other women at Christmas, that kind of thing."

Dana looked around the room for something to write on, her face dark with panic. He held up a firm hand to quell the emotional firestorm he knew to be brewing in her well-intentioned psyche. "You *can't* write anything down, Dana. Can't take notes, can't steal files, can't print copies. You're not a PI, yet. You don't have a license or any credentials to speak of. I don't want you or me getting in trouble. I just need some help and don't know where else to turn. Just find out what you can, informally and off the record, and tell me what you know. That's all."

She looked to him for help. "Where do I start?" she asked.

"Find out where the wife gets her hair done. Go there. Bring a pack of cigarettes and a lighter. And some petty cash. You'll need an appointment with her hairdresser. Get her talking. While you're waiting for the perm to take hold or the curls to dry or whatever it is you girls do, beg off for a smoke break. Offer her one. She'll smoke. All hairdressers smoke, or did smoke, or want to smoke, or need a smoke. Get her out back and pump her for gossip. Bring me back what you find and we'll go from there. Sound good?"

Dana nodded, but didn't speak.

Dana *couldn't* speak.

Dana was crying.

Frank stood up, rushing to hug her, but thought twice and stopped just short, leaning his backside on his desk and reaching out a hand to gently grasp her shoulder instead. "...I'm sorry, Frank," she stammered, "it's just no one's ever trusted me with something like this before."

"I trust you, Dana," he said quietly. "Why do you think I hired you?"

He scrambled for a tissue on his desk but found only an old fast-food napkin left over from some take-out lunch he'd sent Dana to get earlier in the week. (At least, he *hoped* it was from this week.) She took it gratefully and, when she was cleaned up, got right to business.

"Now," she said, sniffling, "about that petty cash. Thing is, we don't really have any left. I've been using it for lunch for you and me all week, and your fast food habit's getting pretty expensive. Maybe if you'd let me order off the value menu at Wendy's I could save you a buck or two, but that's not really your style. Plus, these upscale salons can get pretty pricey, and have you seen the price of cigarettes lately?"

Frank smiled, reaching for his wallet.

She'd do just fine.

12

Dana took the proffered cappuccino and sat in the leather wingback chair, making herself comfortable at none other than Mrs. Arthur Ritchey herself's favorite frou-frou salon. Around her sat the plump and pampered of DC's elite. By her count, Dana's fellow customers included no less than a senator's wife, the press secretary's second assistant, and two former Congresswomen. Thank goodness working for a bestselling author and media darling had prepared her for this; otherwise she'd be completely star-struck.

She longed to take a sip of the frothy coffee drink, but her hands were shaking so badly she could hardly lift the oversized, wheat-colored cup. She set it down on top of the latest issue of *European Vogue* instead and crossed her legs primly, glad she'd opted for the casual yet elegant tweed ensemble instead of the aggressive and bossy silk pantsuit she'd briefly considered while getting dressed that morning.

She'd made the appointment at DC's most exclusive salon—a poser hair-cuttery of the highest order aptly named, simply, "Elite"—just after Frank asked her for help in the Alex Ritchey investigation. The booker who'd answered that day had told her it might be "weeks" before she could fit her in, but a last minute cancellation had opened up and she'd called back earlier that same morning to confirm Dana's afternoon appointment with Sylvia Ritchey's personal stylist, Brie.

Now here she sat, nervous and tense and longing for caffeine, as one by one the salon emptied of its famous clientele, appropriately coiffed and pampered. Dana was somewhat surprised to see that, as each matronly senator's wife or just plain senator left the salon, she was promptly followed by her stylist, clutching what looked like a tackle box full of assorted scissors, combs, and gels.

At first she thought the stylists were helping the women to their cars, perhaps even after selling them the contents of their toolboxes to perform similar hair miracles on themselves at home, but after a few minutes, when the stylists never returned and the salon seemed particularly empty, Dana cleared her throat until she got the booker's attention.

"Yes?" asked the particularly nonchalant yet elegant Goth teen behind the counter, her pale finger holding her place in the article on Tim Burton she was reading in that week's issue of *Premiere* magazine.

"Where did everybody go?" Dana asked.

The booker gave Dana her best "are you new here?" eye roll before explaining, "Tonight's the annual Daughters in Politics gala."

When Dana's eyes begged innocence, the young booker sighed and continued. "Every year DC's most powerful women bring their spawn to this big ballroom so they can all preen in front of each other and pose for pictures in tomorrow's *Washington Post* social section. It's kind of like Bring Your Daughters to Work Day, Washington style. The women get their hair done during the day and then rent their stylists out for the afternoon to do their daughters' hair back home. That's why we had an opening for you today. Senator Carlson's wife usually has Brie style her hair, but her daughter insisted on this new gal she read about in *Cosmo*, so the Carlsons flew her in from LA just for the night. Lucky you, right?"

Dana smiled and shrugged. "Lucky me."

The booker glanced at her watch, then back at the row of empty chairs behind her. Soft lighting filled the room from low-slung, exposed bulbs that reflected in shallow pools off the hardwood floors below.

Oddly-shaped mirrors stood in front of each stylist's station, some encrusted with fake jewels and others in simple bleached wood frames, while old-school dental-style chairs clashed with the post-modern surroundings in an entirely intentional way. Like every hip place Dana had ever been to—and there hadn't been that many, but just enough to draw a worthy comparison—Elite *looked* a lot cooler than it actually was.

"Brie should be out any minute," the booker said, hanging a black-nailed finger over her black-clad shoulder and flipping her thick black hair in the process, "and you're our last appointment of the day. Would you mind if I cut out early? I mean, the small talk's been great and all but there's a new showing at this super little gallery over at Georgetown and my boyfriend's unveiling his latest painting, so...."

Dana stood, uncertain of what the booker was asking even as she assured her, "Sure, sure, that's cool. I'll just wait for Brie and...."

The booker was already at the door, a ratty black messenger bag covered in snarky, retro 80s buttons—"I Want My MTV," "Girls Just Wanna Have Fun," "Judd Nelson Rocks!"—slung low over her sloped shoulders. Candy cane striped white and black socks and rubber soled army boots completed her Adams Family persona. "I'll just lock up so nobody bugs you and Brie can let you out later. Have fun!"

Dana heard the double door locks click shut and the booker's brand new Vespa scooter parked on the sidewalk out front start up and sputter away. She stared at her tepid cup of cappuccino and was just relaxed enough to reach for it when a tall, lanky model wannabe emerged from between two Marilyn Monroe shower curtains, each one bearing the matching half of Marilyn's face.

"Would the cool, funkiness never stop?" Dana wondered to herself as the sexy stylist sauntered her way, clear vinyl heels echoing off the polished blond wood of the floor beneath her.

"Hi," she said breathlessly, as if she'd just run a marathon or, perhaps, had sex. "You must be my four o'clock. I'm Brie, sorry I'm late, but I had an outcall this morning for…."

"The Daughters in Politics gala," Dana said, eager to show off her new knowledge. "I know all about it." She stood up and shook Brie's outstretched hand; it was cold to the touch and wrinkled far beyond what she imagined to be Brie's 20, maybe 21 years.

Her hair was attractively spiky, two words Dana never thought she'd use in the same sentence together but which aptly described the funky, feminine look that was so anti-glam as to be ultra-glam. Brie's eyes were of the darkest blue and her lips wore a light, pale gloss. They hid crooked teeth that pressed against them, making them fuller than they might have looked had her parents splurged on braces, a modern asset they perhaps never intended but one which Brie now enjoyed. Her nose was nondescript, her cheekbones predictably high, and the high heels, faded jeans, and Betty Boop halter top she wore made her seem right at home in the poser environs of the droll Elite salon.

"Come on back," she offered breezily, turning on her heel and revealing a pleasantly plump derriere that gave Dana hope. The lacy band of her black thong panties peaked out over the top of her low-slung jeans, making Dana feel old and dried up in her weekday "granny panties."

"Listen," Brie said over the tapping of her heels, "I don't

normally do this, but it's been a long day and there's nobody else here so, do you mind if I have a glass of wine with you?"

Dana began to protest—true, she *had* taken a cab but she was supposed to meet her fiancé for dinner later and knew he wouldn't approve if she beat him to happy hour, by a few hours no less—but then thought better of herself. Maybe this was one of those super-duper spy tests, you know, like when the hookers ask their johns to say something dirty or fork over the cash first so they know they're not really a cop.

"I was going to insist," Dana said easily, as if perhaps she'd been a private investigator—or pampered salon patron—all her life.

Brie got her settled in the padded chair and then busied herself with pouring two glasses of white wine from a red bottle. Like the crooked ruby bottle itself, the glasses were equally funky, all thick glass and colored rhinestones on the stem, and when Brie clinked her glass in a toast—"to great hair and better boyfriends"—she did so with an affected air that sent a splash of wine onto Dana's ring finger.

Dana took a sip out of the funky glass; it was the best wine she'd ever tasted. She took another sip right away to make sure her taste buds weren't fooling her. It was so dry as to evaporate off the tongue, with just enough vanilla but not too much, and an aftertaste that, like cocaine, left one wanting more.

Brie smirked. "Nice, huh? It's from Chile, a little boutique winery down there. So boutique they had to open up a bed and breakfast next to the vineyard to pay the bills. The ambassador's wife comes in once a week for a facial and a frost and won't drink anything else. I guess they stayed there one summer and she couldn't get enough. Her husband has three cases shipped here every month. Courtesy of the good people of Chile, natch. If they only knew...."

Brie sipped quietly, but steadily, with her left hand while she let her right hand tousle and toy with Dana's unruly mop. "Let me guess," she said, once her glass was to the halfway mark, "Hair Cuttery. No, no, Supercuts. Am I right? I can spot their Wal-Mart scissors anywhere."

Dana blushed and took a heady sip of the luxurious wine to overcompensate for her white trash roots. "You were right the first time," she admitted sheepishly from the bowl of her wine glass. "There's one right next door to my bank so, every other payday, I just pop in for a rinse and a cut. Not a good idea, huh?"

"Not if you want to keep your hair past thirty it isn't," Brie said with a tone that said she suspected Dana might already be thirty after all. Oh, the horror. "So, why the upgrade? What brings a Hair Cuttery girl up to Elite standards?"

Dana almost choked on her wine, and the glass wasn't anywhere near her lips! She hadn't thought Brie was even listening to her. Now she'd have to come up with a reason why she was suddenly taking the leap from a $13.99 cut and dry to a $130 highlight and set. Luckily, Brie's face was buried in her funky wine glass as Dana stammered, "O-o-ooooh, my fiancé and I are celebrating our one-year anniversary tonight, so...."

"Where are you going?" Brie asked automatically, no doubt assuming Dana was going to reel off one from a dozen frou-frou DC eateries favored by the jet set.

This time, Dana had a ready answer: "He said it was a surprise."

Brie giggled. "How romantic," she sighed, noting Dana's mostly empty wine glass. She disappeared to the dorm fridge under the coffee machine and brought back the imported white wine, pouring them off a long, hefty draught before setting the ruby red bottle on her already cluttered work station. "This calls for another toast."

As Dana dutifully clinked glasses again, Brie chirped, "To anniversaries, may you have one every year."

The irony struck Dana halfway through her sip and she snorted loudly into the oversized wine glass. At last the distracted stylist got down to work and the two discussed what Brie would do to offset the damage done by Hair Cuttery over the years. Alternately they sipped, talked, and sipped some more, before Brie finally picked up a pair of trimming shears and set to work creating Dana's "new look."

Just before she got to the bottom of her second glass of wine, Dana met Brie's cobalt blue eyes in the mirror and asked the question that would make or break her so-called investigation. "So, how long have you been working here?"

Brie took an exaggerated moment, thinking back—she was the type of stylist who had to pause from working on your hair prior to answering each question—before answering, "This will be year number three, I believe. Closer to four than three, actually."

"Wow," Dana mock-marveled. "You must have seen some living history walk through these doors, huh?"

"Oh, girl, you wouldn't believe," Brie bragged, just as Dana hoped she might. "Senators, their wives, Congresswomen, Congressmen, their mistresses, the talking heads you see on TV every Sunday, their wives, *their* mistresses.... I should write a book someday."

Dana smiled. It was on the tip of her tongue to say, "I've got just the man to help you do that," but she didn't. Instead, she cleared her throat, took a swig of wine, and said, "I hear you do Arthur Ritchey's wife. What's her name?"

Brie snapped her scissors shut and smiled, but not entirely pleasantly, as if perhaps Dana had overstepped. Dana smiled; she'd heard of lawyer-client privilege before, even doctor-patient, but stylist-client? "Where'd you hear that?" the stylist asked, not entirely sure she wanted her client list to be public knowledge.

Dana had a ready answer for that one, too. She'd already done a google search on Sylvia Ritchey who had, in fact, mentioned the salon—and even the stylist—in a two-year-old puff piece she had to pay $1.99 to read from the *Post* archives. "Something I read in the *Washington Post* last year and filed away for future reference. Guess it came in handy."

Brie seemed to breathe a sigh of relief but, instead of continuing with her haircut opened up another bottle of wine instead. "Do you mind?" she asked, even as she topped off Dana's third glass.

Dana shrugged with an exaggerated "Who? Me?" air. Brie cocked her head, glass in hand, and said, "Your turn."

"For what?" Dana asked.

Brie nudged Dana's thigh with her knee. "The toast, silly. It's your turn to make one."

Dana smiled and knew just what to say: "To new stylists, and all the fresh DC gossip they can supply!"

Brie snorted over her funky wineglass before tossing half of its contents into her gullet. "So," she asked, setting down her scissors and leaning back lazily against her work station, exposing a belly button ring beneath the frayed hem of her halter top. "Where should I start? The husbands, the wives, or the mistresses?"

"Oooh," Dana said, hardly believing her luck. "That's an easy one: the *mistresses*!"

13

The Sniper sat in the stiff wooden chair and waited for the water in the shower to stop running. On his lap was the antique pistol from the day's earlier altercation at the low-rent cantina, since modified with a homemade silencer of his own design—a toilet paper roll stuffed tight with cotton balls and ringed with duct tape; crude but effective.

On the table for two beside him sat a money counting machine and stacks of hundred dollar bills, both counted and stacked, and uncounted and disorderly. It never entered his mind to take a single one of them. This gig had never been about money, even the anonymous kind. Instead he sat stock still, watching the light of the day retreat across the room as shadows grew taller and taller on the roughhewn wooden floor of Arnold "Arnie" Kinsey's rented room.

Much like his victim before him, the Sniper wore flip-flops, a garish floral bathing suit, and a cheap white T-shirt bearing the slogan "One Tequila! Two Tequila! Three Tequila! *Floor*!!!" The throwaway backpack at his feet was filled with a beach towel, some assorted tools of the trade just in case, and of course the leftover makings from his silencer—half a bag of cotton balls and most of a roll of duct tape.

He'd spent the bulk of the afternoon pretend-sunning himself on the private beach in front of Kinsey's hotel, luxuriating on the soft white sand and languishing in the midday heat as the sun kissed the muscles of his six-pack abs and coconut-oiled biceps.

To keep up appearances, he dutifully accepted more than a couple of frozen umbrella drinks from the copper-skinned cabana boy, tipping him generously enough to keep him coming but not so generously that he'd remember him past the end of his day shift or, for that matter, when the Federales came around asking questions about the gringo victim later that week.

The Sniper's thick, wraparound sunglasses might have been a tad severe for a man his age, but they were still stylish enough to pass without notice and—once modified with more reflective material on the inside than on the outside—more than suitable for his purpose. In the left corner of the left lens he had a partial view of Kinsey's room, where the warped French doors with their faded curtains had been propped open ever since his morning constitutional earlier that day.

He knew from watching his subject for the last 72-hours that Kinsey liked to take a leisurely afternoon shower before ambling down to the hotel restaurant overlooking the sea, where he would order precisely three top-shelf margaritas—on the rocks, no salt—before dining on the Honcho Hombre Combo Platter, a nauseating assortment of clichéd Mexican specialties no native would go within a mile of and few tourists ever ordered twice.

At precisely 3:15 Kinsey had appeared at the French doors, taken an appreciative whiff of the redolent salt air, and then shut the doors gracefully, one of the white curtains catching in the crack and flapping intermittently in the lazy ocean breeze. The Sniper's stomach had fluttered at the sight of his prey and he'd forced himself to finish his vacation drink slowly so as not to arouse suspicion from the other sunbathers.

After an appropriate amount of time—Kinsey needed to get in the shower first, after all—he had picked himself up, dusted himself off, packed up his gear and stumbled past the cabana boy, receiving an appreciative if pandering nod on his way up the splintery wooden steps, past the pristine aqua pool, and into the arched hallway that led to a claustrophobic inner corridor featuring the front doors of eight of the hotel's 16 rooms.

He'd found Kinsey's room—#12—and jimmied the cut-rate lock in under a minute. Slipping his tools back into his backpack, he'd stepped into the room to hear the water running in the tiny bathroom before breathing a quiet sigh of relief.

Since then, he'd been staring at the fingerprint of sand sitting soft and white on the darkening skin of his sunburned thigh. There was sand in the crack of his ass and saltwater drying in his ear, and he ached for the cool wash of a frosty *cerveza* to offset the sickeningly sweet piña coladas from the beach.

There was no nervousness in his stomach, no accelerated beating of his heart, no tapping of his foot on the solid wooden floor. Kinsey was a number in the middle of a to-do list, nothing more, nothing less. He must pay, and the Sniper was there to collect what was owed.

The gun was hot and heavy in his lap, and just as he considered standing up to get a drink of water from the outdated kitchen sink, Kinsey's shower water ended with the squeaking of the faucet and the rattling of ancient pipes overhead. Kinsey did not sing in the shower, nor afterward, as some of the Sniper's victims had, and the sound of first one foot, then the other, slapping moistly onto the mildewed tile of the bathroom floor was nearly deafening.

The Sniper could no longer shift in his chair or move his feet, for fear of detection. Now all he could do was sit and wait while Kinsey dried himself off, one pink, fuzzy limb at a time. A pair of crisp linen pants and a garish but expensive floral shirt were laid out on the bed in preparation for the night's festivities, as were some dirty boxer shorts and a pair of pricey leather sandals.

Kinsey remained silent through his post-shower ministrations as the Sniper tried to picture him combing his hair and splashing on cologne in front of the water-stained mirror. Most victims turned the TV on while they were in the shower, not wanting to feel so alone as they dressed; others found their favorite station on the radio and listened to that instead. But Kinsey seemed content with his own company, and nary a whistle nor a hum left his mouth until his bare feet slapped on the tile and he ambled out into the hallway and turned toward the Sniper.

The bullet met him dead in the chest, where it had a better chance of passing through his heart and out his back as opposed to getting caught up and ricocheting around the skull which, as the Sniper had found, was surprisingly strong. Kinsey let out a gasp.

Over the years the Sniper had learned there was little drama in his victim's death scenes. Very few final words and even fewer histrionics. That might have had something to do with the fact that he was a sniper, typically killing people from yards away, but he suspected it had more to do with all those bullshit Hollywood movies and their sappy actors taking star turns while fake blood oozed out from their fake wounds and fake tears spilled from between their contact lenses.

In reality, death was more like a thud than a bang; you were there one minute and gone the next. The life force was a fleeting, fragile thing; one minute you could be splashing on cologne and looking forward to that first margarita of the evening, and the next there's a strange man sitting next to your bundles of money, pointing a smoking toilet paper roll at your bare chest.

Satisfying it was.

Glamorous it most certainly was not.

Kinsey spun like a top, his chest a flushing geyser, sputtering blood-splatter shoulder-high on the otherwise crisp, white walls. The result was like a piece of artwork, something some poser protégé of Andy Warhol might have done back in the 80s. Then the old man took a dive, his nose breaking like a dry twig as he fell face first onto the unforgiving and thirsty Mexican tile.

Blood continued to ooze from his chest as the Sniper shuffled over in his flip-flops and located the spent bullet, flattened like a mushroom and lying half-in, half-out of the thick wooden door. He pried it loose with a souvenir penknife-slash-keychain and pocketed it in the swim trunks he would leave behind in the ocean later that night.

The bullet really didn't matter; he wasn't avoiding detection as much as he was hampering the investigation. Soon enough the victims would pile up, and the Feds—dumb as they were—would add one to the other. He had others on his list; he only hoped he could get to them all by the time they got to him.

He shrugged off the self-doubt and got back to work, checking himself in the mirror and noting that the blood he'd managed to get on himself didn't stand out too much. The smear on his shirt blended in well with his garish tourist slogan and of course his floral baggies were vibrant shades of red and yellow. The bottom of his flip-flops were leaving big fat marks on the smooth, copper-colored tile, but it could hardly be avoided.

He wiped a small teardrop of blood from his cheek with the back of his hand and strode through the room to throw the French doors wide open. It wasn't uncommon for guests to leave their doors open at night, and Kinsey always had. Besides, the ocean air would keep the body cooler longer, and if the maid stayed away for another day, so much the better. If she didn't, no biggie; he'd be long gone by then anyway.

He ambled through the open doors as big as you please, emerging onto a small patch of grass that many of the guests used as a short-cut to the pool. By the time he reached the sun-bleached deck he was glad to see the grass had washed the blood from his footprints. He continued past a handful of dedicated sunbathers out past the cabana bar and onto the sand.

His waiter from before was gone and it was just as well; now he could saunter unmolested down the beach, his backpack slung over one shoulder, the thick old gun weighing it down as he found a small bar too rustic for the tourists and too pricey for the locals.

He found a seat on the mostly empty deck and ordered his first cold beer of the evening. There he would sit, reliving the afternoon, until at last the sun set and the moon rose and the bar patrons began to stumble home, alone or in boozy pairs. He would be one of them, shuffling down the beach for a midnight swim and, after looking around for witnesses and finding none, he would stride into the small, rippling waves and disrobe, foot by precious foot.

The backpack would go first, sinking swiftly to the bottom, and then would come the flip-flops, the ridiculous trunks and the insulting T-shirt. He would drown himself in the curative saltwater, washing away gunpowder and blood and sweat and beer and the heady funk of a kill gone well.

He would emerge, strapping and naked, his skin alternating between shades of blue and silver in the moonlight as he strode eight steps up the beach to a particularly prickly shrub where he had hidden another backpack earlier that morning. Inside would be a change of clothes, another set of ID, his plane ticket, some petty cash, and the number of a Canadian bank account to which he'd wired himself $4,000 dollars earlier in the week.

He would enjoy the feel of the sand between his toes—and even in the crack of his ass—as he shuffled through the sleepy little Mexican town to the bus stop, where in the morning a shabby old school bus, looking vaguely like something out of a *Partridge Family* episode, would take him to the airstrip and his next job.

Looking down from the window of his six-seater puddle-jumper he would try—and try hard—not to say something stupid like, *"Hasta la vista,* baby." He would try, but it might not work. It just seemed like the right thing to do, and besides, no matter the profession, he was still just a kid after all.

Just a kid trying to make his way home.

14

Vinny was buying his wife, Tina, and their two boys souvenirs in the gift shop next to his gate at Heathrow airport when his cell phone rang. He pulled it from his pocket quickly, hoping it was Tina, whom he sorely missed, but quickly noting the unregistered DC number instead.

"Smalldeano here," he answered brusquely before he'd even finished flipping the phone open. A dignified gent complete with a bowler hat and umbrella slung over his arm made a face at the intrusion, but Vinny flicked him off and turned around for more privacy.

The reaction might have been a tad severe by tourist standards but by now he'd had it up to here with the English and their manners, not to mention their greasy food, their bad weather, their law enforcement system, their traffic, and their piss-warm beer.

Vinny had always imagined England to be a cozy, dignified country, "cheerio" and "old sport" and all that, but instead he'd found it to be dirty and rude, unkempt and unpleasant. The only fond memory he'd take away from this trip would be Squire, who had dropped him off in front of his gate some two hours earlier and then quickly sped off, a cigarette dangling from his lip and an outstretched arm waving him goodbye through the halfway rolled down window.

Even English goodbyes were cold and abrupt.

Of course, he didn't blame the swift departure. No doubt

Squire would have hell to pay once he got back to the squad room, where the locals would give him plenty of reasons to regret the kindness he had shown Vinny over the last 48 hours.

"Smalldeano?" barked the newly familiar voice of his direct supervisor, Special Director Flaherty. "Where are you right now?"

"Gift shop. Heathrow. Souvenirs for the wife, kids. Why?"

"Make 'em light and portable, sonny. Try magnets, that's what I always get 'em. Thin, flat, and portable. You should see my wife's collection. Got so many you can barely see the refrigerator anymore, if you know what I mean. Listen, kid, I know you just now got over your jet lag, but I'm afraid we've got a new case for you. I won't go into it over the phone but it could be related to…."

"Related?" Vinny asked. "To what? England?"

"It's not 100 per cent yet, Smalldeano, but it's looking that way. Sixty-ish businessman, Caucasian, American, low-rent hotel, cash-counting machine on the table, single bullet wound to the chest, through and through, no bullet, no evidence, no witnesses, no leads."

"Sounds related all right," Vinny muttered, putting down his coffee mug for Tina and T-shirts for the boys and snatching up three magnets instead. Each one had a picture of Big Ben on the front.

"Like I said," Flaherty continued, sounding impatient or rushed or both. "I've got a ticket in your name waiting on you at the Air Mexico counter. Flight leaves in four hours. Sorry, it's the best I could do. We've got a field office down there. I'll have a dossier waiting on a desk for you, so you shouldn't have the same muck-up you found back in England. Sorry about that, me boy; there's only so much I can do from the home office, if you catch my drift. Hotel where I've got you staying is only three blocks away, so you won't even need a taxi.

"Call me after you've landed, checked in, and had a chance to read the file. Any hour, day or night. If this is what I think it is, we've got about two good days before the press picks it up. I'll try to buy you three, if I can, but you're gonna have to work fast either way. You up to it, me boy?"

"Aye, aye sir," he said as the gal behind the counter gave him his change from his last stack of pound notes. He needn't have bothered trying to be funny; Flaherty had already hung up.

15

Frank sat on the leather loveseat in the reception area and stared at Dana's new 'do. He didn't know why he preferred the outer office to his own; maybe it was the smooth jazz or the open space or the plants or the magazines or the way the big front door afforded him a quick exit when the walls started closing in. Then again, maybe it was Dana herself.

After a few cocks of his head and a click of his tongue or two, he decided he approved of the new look—and told her so. She blushed quickly and easily, charmingly, starting in the throat and spreading to her forehead, and then said, "Thanks, Frank." Their eyes met, her blush rose even higher, if it were possible, and then she looked quickly down into her lap. She let the acknowledgement hang in the air until Frank prompted, "Tell me more about this Moonglow character."

Dana looked at the notes she'd taken on the taxi ride home after her haircut, scribbled on the back of Brie's business card and, thanks to all those funky glasses of delectable wine, scribbled in a big, loopy scrawl she could barely decipher the next morning.

"I can only tell you what Brie told me, for now, but apparently Mrs. Ritchey—Sylvia is her name—couldn't have children. A woman named Moonglow—a girl, really, since according to Brie she was barely eighteen at the time—was their surrogate, so apparently your Alex Ritchey wasn't actually Sylvia's child, though it's not clear if he was Arthur Ritchey's or not."

"Dollars to donuts it is," Frank said confidently, as if to himself. When Dana's eyebrows arched, he explained. "A guy like Arthur Ritchey is not going to involve a doctor, a lab, a nurse, let alone a hospital or clinic where any number of staff could see him or spot the name on the sperm sample and sell their story to the press. No, he's going with as few witnesses as possible, and I guarantee he fertilized little Moonglow there the old-fashioned way: up close and personal. Cheap hotel room, a bottle of wine, a bouquet of five-dollar daisies, and it's all over but the foreplay. Chances are when you find pictures of this hippy-chick, she will have been one sweet-looking teenager. Blond hair, blue eyes, kewpie doll 'do, a real Goldie Hawn look-alike."

"Goldie Hawn?" Dana asked, unfamiliar with the reference.

Frank shook his head. What was wrong with this generation? "You know," he sighed, using a reference she could better understand. "Kate Hudson's mom?"

Dana nodded, smiling at him condescendingly, as if she were a candy striper visiting him at his nursing home. "Why didn't you say so?"

"Point is," Frank continued, feeling old and out of touch, "this guy has the best of both worlds." Before Dana had a chance to turn up her perky little nose and ask "How so?" Frank answered her, "His wife can't have kids so she gives him permission, hell, she probably flat out *demanded* that he go find a surrogate, and because neither of them can risk the bad press of a test tube baby, he basically gets carte blanche to go out and have an affair. Who even knows if this Moonglow character was his first choice? He might have spent weeks on the project, months even, sampling every nubile young nymph this side of the Potomac. Guy must have been like a kid in a candy store, and all with his wife's blessing."

"Well," Dana said, grimacing at this distasteful little tidbit, "I suppose that could explain why the kid grew up in boarding schools and was raised by nannies, not to mention why Daddio is in here every week for a progress report."

Frank looked at her funny. "Really?" he asked, cocking his head in that way of his. She noticed the gray dancing through his salt and pepper hair and wondered if it was too soon in their relationship to suggest a quick trip to Elite and a seat in Brie's chair. "I would think it would be just the opposite."

Dana shook her head. "Guilt," she surmised, the pupil becoming the teacher. "The mom feels guilty she couldn't have her own child, the father feels guilty he ignored the kid all these years, not to mention the fact that he chose the personal donor method over in vitro fertilization. Now the kid's missing and he's moving heaven and earth to find him."

"Or is he?" Frank asked pointedly.

Now it was Dana's turn to cock her head; the pupil was the pupil again.

"There are about two dozen PIs in DC who are more qualified than I am," Frank explained. Dana opened her mouth to protest but her boss cut her off with a raised hand and a fierce scowl. "Yeah, I know, they may not be as visible as I am, but that's the point. You don't want a famous PI to find your kid; you want a *good* PI. One with connections, a network of informants, a Rolodex fat with guys who will do him favors and show him the short-cuts. You want someone who's been around the block, not the *new* kid on the block.

"My ex-wife had a saying. Whenever I'd come home late and had too good of an excuse, you know, all the angles covered and every second accounted for, credit card receipts, time stamps, movie stubs, the works, she'd always smirk and say, 'Methinks one doth protest too much.' I used to hate that saying and I never even really understood it until just now. Right this very minute.

"I've got no proof, not yet anyway, and there's probably not a soul on this earth who would agree with me right now except you, Dana, but methinks Arthur Ritchey protests too much."

16

Dana found Moonglow's last known address later that day and was up and on the road early the next morning. She smiled as she headed out of D.C., proud of what she'd managed to accomplish in just a few short days since becoming Frank's unofficial "partner." Here she was heading out of town to locate the surrogate of one of America's richest men, and she didn't even have her PI's license yet, though Frank assured her he was "looking into it."

The run-down trailer park—or, she wondered, was that redundant?—was located just south of the Virginia border, and she found lot #228 just before noon. It looked lived-in and appropriately hippy-ish for a woman named Moonglow, complete with rainbow pinwheels spinning silently in the carefully-tended flower garden and potted ferns nestled in crocheted baskets dangling from a rusty white awning, but the tiny little two-door import in the single parking space was decidedly capitalistic.

A wind chime rustled as Dana made her way up the rusty front steps, where a faded welcome mat greeted her functional blue pumps. She smoothed down her navy skirt and tugged on her crisp white blouse to flatten out the wrinkles that had formed in the back during her long drive south from DC. There was no doorbell so she knocked, once, twice, firmly, noting that the hollow door seemed flimsy enough to kick in, should it come to that.

It didn't; Moonglow answered on the fourth knock, looking decidedly, well, sunny. She had a round, oval face; not fat, exactly, but…fleshy. She looked like she didn't get much exercise or, for that matter, too much sun. Her skin was almost translucent, pale, papery and see-through, though her mouth was smiling around smoker's yellow teeth and lighting up pale green eyes in the process.

Although by Dana's calculations the woman could only have been in her mid- to late forties, she wore an old woman's house dress and fuzzy pink slippers. In her hand was a half-smoldering cigarette.

"Oh dear," she said as her hands instinctively rose to her unkempt hair. "I so wish I'd known I was going to have visitors today. I must look a complete and utter fright."

Dana could have kicked herself for not calling first, and she stood on the front stoop stammering her way through an introduction. All that time in the car and she hadn't even come up with a good reason to interview Moonglow!

Luckily, Frank had lent her his ID card. She flashed it now, and spoke quickly as she bluffed, "Ma'am, my name is Dana Gregorian and I'm a private investigator working with Frank Logan Investigations. I…."

"You mean that writer Frank Logan?" the woman interrupted.

Dana nodded brusquely as Moonglow uttered, "Come in, come in. I so love his books, although I have to wait until they come out in paperback before I can afford them. A little pricey in hardcover, wouldn't you say? Although as his assistant, you probably get them for free. This isn't about those neighbors I had last year, is it? The ones who disappeared in the middle of the night? I always thought they looked kind of suspicious, between you, me and the lamppost. Rumor had it the husband killed the wife and then left town. No one's ever seen him since. What did you say this was about again, dear?"

"I didn't, ma'am," Dana rushed as the woman led her into a surprisingly spacious living room. "But it's in reference to your relationship with a man named Arthur J. Ritchey."

Moonglow stopped dead in her tracks. The cigarette dangled at her side, burning up from her suddenly trembling hand as the smoke swirled around her body like an anaconda wrapping around its prey.

"Oh dear," she finally said after what must have surely been a full minute of the two women standing stock still in her living room, "I can't say as I'm surprised to see you, but I sure hoped that I'd have a few more years to prepare!"

Moonglow turned slowly, her cigarette rising to her dry, pink lips as she admitted, "But then, I've had all this time and look at me: still as unprepared as if it all happened just yesterday. Sit, sit, I suppose we have much to talk about, you and I."

Moonglow took a well-worn, faux leather reclining chair and Dana sat in the proffered love seat across from her. As the older woman fidgeted to get comfortable, Dana quickly took in the room: mass-produced, cheaply-framed art prints covered the walls, mostly of the full moon, Native American, howling wolf variety.

If only I had a black light, Dana thought to herself.

There were some plastic plants and a TV but, other than the recliner on one side of the room and the seat upon which Dana rested, there wasn't much furniture. She did notice a large-print *TV Guide* on the coffee table in front of her, a yellow highlighter resting closely nearby. It reminded her of the way her new husband carefully planned out their evening TV time together, a week in advance.

"Now," Moonglow said somewhat firmly from across the

room, "what is it you want to know?" Before Dana could answer, the older woman gestured toward the kitchen area at the back of the double-wide. "I'm sorry, where are my manners? Could I offer you something to drink? Some tea, perhaps? Or a ginger snap or two?"

Dana smiled and said, "No, and please, don't apologize. I'm sure me showing up like this today must be quite a shock to you."

Moonglow settled back into her chair, easing the thin material of her faded butterfly housecoat down across her thighs over and over again. Dana realized it must have been a nervous gesture. "Not so much a surprise," she admitted, "though certainly a disappointment. The Ritcheys and I had been so careful to keep it a secret, you see."

Dana nodded. *I'm sure they did*, she thought. Out loud she said, "Did you ever meet Sylvia Ritchey? I mean, face to face? Up close and personal?" She felt like she should have a notebook out but she'd read somewhere that made people feel uncomfortable. Besides, she hadn't used one at the Elite salon, and look how well that had gone. Why mess with a good thing, right? Or as her father used to say, "If it ain't broke, why fix it?"

Moonglow nodded before tamping out her cigarette in an overflowing orange ashtray on the end table next to her chair. "Just that once," she explained, blowing out a thick plume of smoke that threatened to waft Dana's way, "in the hospital. She came to pick up little Alex, you see. I gave him willingly. It was my choice. Not one I'm proud of, you see, but a choice just the same."

Dana nodded. She looked nervously around the living room. Things were going so well. She'd never imagined Moonglow would be so…divulging. And yet talking to Brie had been so much easier. What she wouldn't give for a glass of wine!

Moonglow seemed to sense her hesitance. She cocked her head to one side, her limpid yellow hair following her gesture as it spilled off her shoulders and onto the arm of the chair. "You seem awful young to be doing this, dear. If you don't mind me saying so, that is. Maybe it would help if I just told you the story."

Dana nodded, stopping herself from breathing a huge sigh of relief. But only barely.

Moonglow took several minutes to get situated. First she located a faux leather cigarette case that matched her faux leather chair. From inside she plucked a long, thin cigarette and a shiny silver lighter with a turquoise oval in the center. Dana thought it matched the pseudo-southwestern décor of the trailer's interior: the Native American wall-hangings, the Arizona-themed lamp, the pewter cowboy riding a pewter horse on one corner of the coffee table.

Finally Dana heard the flick of Moonglow's Bic and the swift, expert inhale of a lifelong smoker. Thin paper sizzled and nicotine burned and at last the woman spoke: "I was a student at Georgetown when we met. Pre-med. It was the early 80s and I was taking some business course or another because my counselor told me how competitive the field of medicine was going to be. 'You'll need a business background to stand out,' she said, as if being a woman wasn't enough. So I took one, something about entrepreneurship or business capital or God knows what.

"Arthur Ritchey was a guest lecturer one night. A decade or so older, not very handsome, but a born talker. He and some friends had just formed some company and were flush with a big infusion of cash, so I suppose that made him an entrepreneur of some sort or another. So we listened, so young and impressionable, and as Georgetown was wont to do, they had a social gathering afterward. Plenty of tea and little cakes and cucumber sandwiches and such. Arthur talked some more, I was intrigued, and by the time we looked up from talking everyone else had drifted away. I'd never been so embarrassed in my life!

"Well, one thing led to another and he asked me out. We didn't sleep together that night, I assure you. My parents might have raised me on a commune in the middle of the southwest, but they didn't raise a fool. He wined and dined me, and it wasn't until he told me his wife couldn't have children that he made me what he called a 'business proposition.'

"That's what it was, really. I was never into him romantically or anything. I'd been raised in a family of eighteen children and I thought it was a crime not to be able to have one of your own. So I agreed. Simple as that. Now here you are, looking under a rock for some private investigator. Can you tell me, why would Frank Logan be looking for me? And if he is, why isn't he here himself?"

Dana cocked her head. "Mrs...."

"*Ms.*," Moonglow corrected her pleasantly, if firmly. "Ms. Moonglow Magnolia, that's the name they gave me."

"Ms. Magnolia," Dana continued, "haven't you heard? Alex Ritchey is...missing. Frank Logan is the private investigator Arthur Ritchey hired to find him."

Moonglow looked upset, but not as upset as she had when she heard why Dana was there. She looked up from smoothing her housecoat across her lap and admitted, "I finally sprung for cable." She pointed to the *TV Guide* for emphasis. "I suppose I've been too busy catching up on *All in the Family* re-runs to pay much attention to the news."

Dana nodded. She understood. It had only really been "news" for a few days anyway. Either Arthur Ritchey had a lot of pull at the networks or he'd purchased most of them, because after those first few days the case quickly rotated out of the news cycle. Maybe Moonglow had been busy installing cable that weekend. Or maybe she just didn't want Dana to know the truth.

"I have to ask, Ms. Magnolia...."

"Please," the older woman interrupted, "call me Moonglow. Everyone does. I know it sounds silly to a young, powerful, modern woman of your generation, but nobody's called me Ms. Magnolia since I left college. Bitter memories there, I'm sure you understand."

"Did you ever go back?" Dana asked. "I mean, after you had Arthur Ritchey's son?"

Moonglow shook her head. "I was well compensated, you see. I didn't want to be, hadn't asked for it, just so you know. But like I said, I wasn't a fool, either. Arthur deposited a monthly stipend in my bank account. Still does, for that matter. The money made it possible for me to do things I'd always wanted to do. Join the Peace Corps, work for the Red Cross, that sort of thing. I use the trailer here as my base of operations and move on when I get bored. It's no replacement for my son, mind you, but it keeps me busy when the nights get too long, if you catch my drift."

Dana nodded. "So Arthur Ritchey continues to pay you to this day?"

Moonglow nodded somewhat defiantly. "I never asked, mind you. He insisted. Frankly, I think that was all Sylvia's doing. It was horribly shameful for her, you see, to not be able to have children. Don't know why; it's purely natural. Some can, some can't. Those who can, help those who can't, that's what I always say. Anyway, I think she pushed for it, plus she didn't approve of the way the whole affair was handled, and partly the stipend was her way of getting back at Arthur for putting her—for putting *us*—through all that."

"Us?" Dana pried.

Moonglow sighed and lit another cigarette off the last before explaining. "The minute I agreed to be a surrogate, Arthur set me up in one of those little brownstones around the corner from Georgetown. Had it all furnished for me, or so I thought. Later I learned he'd always kept the place, and probably always would. It was his bachelor pad, you see, and I was but one of his many 'bachelorettes.'

"I lived there for a month or two; he'd come by every Wednesday at precisely 6 p.m. We'd have a drink or two, some dinner, and go to bed. I knew I was pregnant after the first week but I'd been spoiled by then. I waited until the last minute to take a pregnancy test, and the second he found out I'd gotten pregnant he bought me this place and I was 'relocated.' I've been here ever since."

"And after you had Alex," Dana asked, "you and Arthur went your separate ways?"

Moonglow nodded. "Oh yes, he wanted nothing to do with me after that. The checks came, and that was that. Sylvia sent me the loveliest Christmas card that first year, but never again. I think she might have kept doing so, maybe even involved me in Alex's life, if it hadn't been for Arthur."

"Did you ever see him again?"

"Who, Arthur? Yes, just once. He showed up here, unannounced, just like you, and demanded the Christmas card back. Can you believe it? Said he didn't want me to have 'proof' of our relationship."

"Did you give it to him?"

"Of course I did. Arthur can be, how shall I put this, very persuasive."

"But, I mean, you had his child. How did he think he could get all the proof just by re-gifting a Christmas card?"

Moonglow shrugged her nearly non-existent shoulders. "Your guess is as good as mine, dear. But, until now, he has."

"You mean I'm the first person to ever ask you about any of this?"

"First and only."

"Not a reporter, not one of Ritchey's investors, not Alex himself?"

"No, no, and sadly, no. After that day at the hospital, I never saw little Alex again."

Dana was halfway back to DC before she realized the woman had been lying to her.

17

Frank looked at the Caller ID feature on his office phone and blinked twice. He was not a man used to being surprised, nor one for the quick double-take, but to see "blocked" in his digital green window gave him reason to pause.

After all, he'd paid extra to allow *all* calls, and even more to ID the most challenging, a feature offered to only the most elite of DC's citizens, most of them former Federal employees like himself. Very few calls should be blocked, and so he picked up the receiver with hesitance. Only when he heard Vinny Smalldeano's familiar voice did he begin to relax.

"Vinny!" he shouted, glad Dana was out on "assignment" so she couldn't complain about his bellowing into the phone. "Where the hell are you? Sounds like you're down in a hole somewhere?"

"In a manner of speaking," Vinny laughed, his voice somewhat garbled in the translation. "I'm in Mexico, of all places."

"Mexico?" Frank asked, instantly on alert. "What the hell for?"

Vinny quickly ran down the new assignment, though Frank noticed he was careful not to share any vital details over the phone. *Good boy, Vinny*, Frank thought to himself as he tried to read between the lines. *I guess I taught you well after all.*

"So that's what I'm doing in Mexico," Vinny wound down. "Some fun, huh?"

"Hey," Frank remembered, interrupting, "congratulations on the promotion. That Flaherty's not one to hand out compliments, by the way. You must have really impressed him."

"Oh, I dunno," Vinny blushed, "I think he just needed some sucker to tramp around the globe cleaning up his mess. I can't say as if I feel very 'international' or 'elite' at the moment, Frank. I kind of feel pretty stupid, if you know what I mean."

Frank had never heard his old partner so down in the dumps before. Usually the kid was full of piss, vinegar, and gunpowder. Now he was sounding more like kitten tails and cockle shells.

"Hey, kid," Frank guffawed, trying to keep things light. "Pretty and stupid don't always mix, if you get my drift. Relax. You're being too hard on yourself. Listen, these satellite phones aren't always the hottest and you're kinda breaking up, but Flaherty wouldn't have sent you down there if he didn't need you. Sounds like you're chasing some vigilante, if you know what I mean. We can't go into particulars with the unsecure line, I know, but if what I'm hearing is kosher, these guys sound pretty similar."

Frank had hit a nerve. He almost felt the light bulb going off over Vinny's head all the way through the satellite phone. "Yeah, Frank, but the MO's all wrong. Two different victims, two different guns. One long range, one up close and personal. I can't help but feel it's like the Maze Murderer all over again, you know? But I've got no frame of reference. No evidence. The Mexicans are actually cooperating this time, but without any trace from England, I've got nothing to compare what I'm finding here with. It's like finding a needle in a haystack, only the needle's in one country and the haystack's in another!"

Frank laughed aloud. Vinny protested at first, but then he soon caught on. When he finally heard Vinny's recognizable guffaw—it always sounded like something you'd hear in the back of a pizza parlor in Brooklyn after one of the patrons had just told a dirty joke—Frank realized he actually missed Vinny.

Dana was in many ways a "replacement Vinny." Young, smart, quick, alert, funny, not one to put up with his BS or molly-coddle him. Physically, the two couldn't have been anymore different—Vinny with his brash good looks and bulging muscles and Dana with her feminine wiles and thin, athletic grace—but mentally the two challenged him to stay young, alert, and in many ways, alive.

"Hey, Frank, listen," Vinny blurted into the cell phone, sounding like he was going through a tunnel, "the medical examiner just got here so I've got to bolt. It was great catching up. I saw a pay phone outside this little neighborhood cantina. Maybe I'll call you later? We can catch up? Talk about the case for real?"

"Don't make promises to old men you can't keep, Vinny," Frank sighed. "Mexico's not like DC, my boy. You could be there watching the ME take a siesta all day, if you catch my drift. Call me when you can. You know the number. I'm always here."

Perhaps it was the wistfulness in Frank's voice that finally reminded Vinny of his manners. "I'm sorry, Frank, I called up and burned your ear and never asked a thing about your new gig. How's that goin', man?"

"Forget it, kid, too late now. Just go gather your evidence and call me when you can. You'll have plenty of time to listen to me prattle on about early retirement when you've caught this guy and become an international super spy hero. Then again, maybe you won't. Either way, it's a good problem to have."

"F-F-Frank," Vinny squawked, making Frank realize

Vinny hadn't heard a word he said. "F-Frank you're breaking up. Listen, I'll c-c-catch you...."

Vinny's words were gobbled up by static, and then the line was severed with a swift and audible snap. Thousands of miles away, Frank sat cheerfully at his desk, thinking of the old days and reliving past exploits.

If only he could help Vinny in some small way.

18

Vinny closed up the bulky satellite phone and sat on the roughhewn wooden chair outside of Kinsey's room. The French doors were open and the white canvas drapes fluttered in the wind like the ghosts of Cinco de Mayo past.

He sighed and smiled, and then smiled once more. It felt good to talk to Frank; he'd been right to call. He'd lied; the Mexican medical examiner had come and gone hours ago. It was just that Frank sounded so down, so blue, he didn't want to rub it in that he was out living a life, crossing the globe and tracking down an international murderer.

Still, it had been good to talk to the old man. Frank had taught him so much; there was no way Vinny could be jet-setting like this, finding clues where there were none, tying two cases into one, if it weren't for the legendary Frank Logan. Now, though, it felt different.

Frank was sitting on his duff back in DC, listening to jazz and flirting with his secretary, and Vinny was in Mexico, wiping the sweat off his already sunburned brow and trying to figure out why two overweight, overage, under-protected Americans had been gunned down in two entirely different countries, all in the same week.

At first, Vinny had reasoned—had, in fact, hoped—that the English job was an English hit. Some fat-ass American entrepreneur taking too many liberties with an impolite British client. Who else would know you could stand on top of that

Coke sign and fire off two quick rounds without anybody seeing or hearing a peep?

But when Flaherty called to weigh in with this Mexican case, all bets were off. He'd still imagined the two were unrelated until he saw the victim, the money counter, the crisp linen pants and the drawer full of margarita receipts.

The law back in London hadn't been too helpful in the end, but a name and an employer was all Vinny needed to connect the two: Arnold "Arnie" Kinsey, his Mexican victim, and Philip Bronstein, his English victim, had both been founding members and CEOs at SouthCom Digital, LLC, a DC-based provider of digital communications.

Think Verizon—on steroids. These guys were ruthless scavengers, finding and buying small, start-up wireless providers and then adding them to the SouthCom Digital fold, one after the other, until out of nowhere they had risen to rival, and then surpass, their bigger, better-known competitors.

Word had it that they'd since gone global. So was that the connection? Two American businessmen doing business in two foreign companies and getting whacked by two international clients who were insulted by a too-low buyout offer?

Vinny stood up from the chair and took one last look at the azure waters just past the cantina bar and walked back inside Kinsey's room. He saw the outfit still waiting for the night out on the town that never came, saw the masking tape outlining where poor Arnie's body had fallen, and the divot in the big, oversized wooden door where the killer, or killers, had taken out his bullet.

Two CEOS.

One company.

Two countries.

One killer?

Vinny didn't know. He was out of his farm area, out of his home stadium, maybe even out of his league. Killers were killers; it didn't matter what country they were in or what language they spoke, the killing mind was universal. But he was so off-kilter, so jet-lagged and hampered by the hungover feeling that went along with it, he couldn't get his game on; couldn't concentrate.

Only now, with the local officials gone and the curtains rustling in the breeze, could he picture the crime, imagine the killer, and sense the tragedy that had taken place. He couldn't do anything more for Kinsey or, for that matter, his business partner and predecessor, Philip Bronstein.

But according to their corporate website, SouthCom Digital had two other partners: Arthur P. Murray and Stephen Anderson, not to mention their founder and controlling partner, the world famous Arthur P. Ritchey himself. Were they next? Were they uninvolved?

Were they already dead?

Clues were not going to solve this crime for Vinny Smalldeano. But maybe, just maybe, the victims he saved could.

19

Dana had wasted almost three hours driving to DC and back, not to mention the half-hour lunch she'd enjoyed before she realized the hapless hippy had pulled a fast one on her. When she pulled back up to the trailer at lot #228 almost four hours later, she was not surprised to see the little two-door import was gone, leaving behind little more than oil stains in the driveway and skid marks on the road.

Her heart raced as she leapt out of her car and bounded up the metal steps two at a time, but she needn't have rushed. She could have knocked all night and no one would answer. She had known it the minute she pulled a U-turn just past the Virginia/DC border. Had known it the whole time she was speeding back, watching the gas level on her dashboard creep closer to "E" and hoping against hope she could make it there in time.

Dana had never broken into a home before, let alone a mobile home, but she knew that barging in the front door wouldn't exactly be the right way to go about things. Instead she crept around back, grateful for Moonglow's green thumb and the row of potted sunflowers that formed a protective barrier between the back of her trailer and the front of another. Between the thick green stalks and the fat yellow heads, Dana had a good layer of subversion in which to do her dirty work.

She started by checking out the two windows in her line

of vision, finding that, of course, only the one that would require her to stand on a nearby wheelbarrow and teeter-totter on her navy pumps was open. After five minutes of writhing and wiggling, she finally found herself standing in Moonglow's shower.

It was dry, signaling that the hippy hadn't bathed before she left. An equally dry sink told her she hadn't brushed her teeth or washed her face, either, though her toothbrush holder was empty and the medicine cabinet above the sink was half-open and half-empty as well. She'd left behind only a single bottle of aspirin and two jars of face cream.

The bedroom looked as if it had been ransacked, and six empty hangers hung in the closet next to six that held nearly identical housecoats. A bare space on the shelf above the dresses told her that the black suitcase resting there was missing its twin.

The rest of the trailer, already mostly empty and feeling barren anyway, felt particularly eerie as the sun drew near to the horizon and shadows crossed the carpet at Dana's feet like the ghosts of old affairs. She checked the fridge to find it, like the rest of the trailer, half-empty. The pantries were likewise half-bare.

There were some books on the floor, scattered, half-open and leaning up against a now half-empty bookshelf. They were mostly romances, and Moonglow must have only packed her favorites. Dust patterns on this table or that revealed where a picture frame or favored statue had been tossed into the fleeing hippy's luggage. Only the back bedroom remained untouched.

Dana felt tears spring to her eyes as she spotted a little boy's room, with trains on the bedspread and a blue and white striped engineer's cap hanging off one corner. The pillows were shaped like cabooses, red and soft, and a lamp on the nightstand poked out of a large shiny engine. She had even painted a train starting on one wall and steaming toward the other; it ran right over the little boy's train bed.

A caboose frame on the bureau held not a picture but two tiny footprints. Next to it was a piece of paper folded in the middle and propped up on both ends. On the front it said simply, "Dana."

Inside she wept as she read the three short lines written in an old hippy's hasty scrawl:

Dear Girl,

Thank you for uncovering my secret. Now perhaps I can live the rest of my life out in the open. Perhaps, one day, Alex will finally come find me as you did.

My deepest gratitude,

Moonglow Magnolia

Dana refolded the letter and slid it into her breast pocket. She thought of Moonglow out in the open, sharing her story with waitresses and truck drivers and Red Cross volunteers as she crisscrossed the world. She thought of a man like Arthur Ritchey and how much he was paying her boss to look for his son.

Moonglow's son.

How much more would he pay to have his mother silenced?

On her way out of the trailer, Dana crept back into the

little boy's room and grabbed the frame holding the two little footprints. She had a feeling she might be needing them one day. Not in case Alex Ritchey ever came back. But in case his father did.

20

The Sniper drank his Molson Golden and watched the dazzling lights of Vancouver twinkle outside of his rented hotel room. He'd never given Canada a second thought; never wanted to travel there or work there or certainly pull a job there, but this city had changed his mind.

He'd always pictured Mounties and bacon and beer when he thought of Canada, so the size and sophistication of downtown Vancouver had startled him. How American of him to think that only the United States could have bright, well-lit walkways and lush, grassy dog parks and lively, eclectic bistros and five-star cuisine.

For whatever it was worth, for however long it might last, this job had shown him one thing: there was, in fact, a big, wide world beyond his country's borders, and it was rich and inviting and deserved a second look.

Maybe, if he lived long enough, he'd come back for pleasure and not business.

Of course, as big as Vancouver was, there was still no way for his prey to hide. It had taken awhile, but he'd finally tracked Arthur P. Murray down to Room #1356 at the downtown Sheraton, a glittering monster of chrome and glass into which he was peering at that very moment.

Arthur was a fan of the ladies. Ladies of the night, that is. As the Sniper watched, a woman tottered into the room on teetering heels and an obvious high of some sort. Booze, coke, smack, yellow jackets, tar, heroin, crank, meth, whatever; it made little difference to the Sniper.

What *did* thrill him, of course, was the power over life or death. From six stories above and a city street between them, with a crack in the window and a rifle with enough power to zoom in on the complimentary bar of soap in the bathroom, he enjoyed sparing the hooker. Would she ever know her life had been in danger that night? Would she ever appreciate the fact that she'd been seconds, millimeters, a hair's breath away from biting the big one?

He doubted it.

Live and let live; that was his motto. Unless, of course, you found your way into the crosshairs of his digitally-enhanced night vision scope, that is. Still, the hooker seemed harmless enough. High-priced but not high-class; expensive but not exclusive. He'd watched Arthur live the high-life for the last 48 hours, and this was girl #3 for the feisty old fart. Meanwhile, the room hadn't been serviced in days, most likely before the Sniper had even gotten a bead on him. Room service trays and condom wrappers littered the floor as the old man fished a fresh bottle of champagne from out of a silver bucket. The Sniper watched through the scope and wondered if old Arthur knew his time was up, or if this was the way he lived back home, too. His portfolio was thin, so he was making it up as he went along.

Still, he had to marvel at these guys. They didn't like to go far. When he'd first taken on the assignment, he'd thought that traveling abroad would mean a few more exotic locations. France, Turkey, Greece, maybe even Norway or Sweden. The Middle East, Russia…*something*.

So far, he'd barely needed his passport!

Canada. Pretty as it could be, sophisticated as it was, he'd hardly call it an exotic port of call. Still, a gig was a gig, and at least this time he could rest his rump on an end chair, leave his high-powered rifle on a tripod, and enjoy a nice, cold Canadian beer while he waited for the high-price hooker to service his target.

Of course, he didn't watch. Couldn't watch. He'd tried the first night, thought it might give him a thrill, but instead it only made him shiver and grimace. So much for the free porn. Now he turned away, counting the seconds on his watch and glad when it was all over a few minutes later.

With the hooker dressed and on her way, the Sniper finished his beer and glanced once again through the precise night scope. The eerie green and yellow of the enhanced digital display was spooky the first few times he'd used it, but over the years he'd gotten used to seeing the world represented through tubes or dials and not always so three-dimensional.

All he really needed to see was a head or a chest anyway; the rest was all just so many details. Arthur P. Murray emerged from his nightly, post-sex shower clad in baggy boxers and an old wife-beater tank top. He looked like a resident in some nursing home, not the head of some multi-billion dollar corporation.

The Sniper shook his head; all that money and no class. He waited until Arthur lay on his bed, but took him before he had time to lift the remote and turn on the television; too much backlight and glare. The blood, when it sprayed from his head, looked like yellow fizz spraying from a green can.

The Sniper chuckled. All of a sudden, he was really thirsty.

21

Vinny Smalldeano stood in room #1356 of the Vancouver Sheraton and felt at home. It wasn't just the English language, sans accent, that made him feel more comfortable, or the relaxed extradition laws, or the nearby FBI field office, or even the helpful nature of Canadian law enforcement.

Vinny Smalldeano finally had a crime scene.

Better yet, he also had a witness.

It was all he could do to concentrate on what the crime scene tech was telling him about "high-velocity spatter" and "time of death" as she pointed to the fine spray of blood and brain spread across the hotel room wall above the victim's headboard like some motley Chinese fan.

Vinny was already a step ahead of her. This was his third "victim scene," though he'd yet to have an actual crime scene. Until now, that is. So far he'd seen his fair share of dead white men: 60-ish, bloated, powerful men who'd suddenly left the states—all within a week of each other, or so his support homework said—and all for four corners of the globe. One to England, another to Mexico, now a third here in Canada, of all places.

Three men, three countries, three different types of gun, but one common thread remained: they all worked for the same company. Scratch that: They all *owned* the same company: SouthCom Digital, LLC.

Vinny only realized he was tapping his left foot when the

crime scene tech rolled her eyes, swabbed one last bit of blood splatter, and smirked at him. "Thus endeth the lesson, Smalldeano," she said. I know you're anxious to get to your crime scene, so rest assured we'll have the analysis of all this material waiting for you back in the lab when you're through across the street. Sure you can find it, big boy? Vancouver's a big city, you know...."

Vinny was already gone. The time for chit-chat and witty cop banter, be it Canadian or Mexican, was long over. He tore down the stairs, out the side door, and into the smaller, but taller, and less exclusive hotel next door. Up the elevator to the 26th floor and onto a hall crowded with uniformed techs scouring every trash chute, ashtray, and wall sconce from one end of the floor to another.

He forced himself to slow down as he reached the door to room #2678, where their sniper had apparently stayed the previous evening. "Smalldeano?" asked a large, rotund senior official at the door. Vinny nodded, prepared to scuffle if need be. Instead, the man simply nodded and stepped aside.

Finally, Vinny thought ruefully as he alighted into a room surprisingly devoid of techies and lab coats, *a little professional courtesy*.

Vinny walked to the center of the room and stood still as a handful of various officials completed their rounds and scurried away. He surveyed the simple room with a practiced eye, listening to the sashay of a fingerprint brush as quiet voices compared angles and measurements.

A middle-aged woman who hadn't seen the sun in years approached him cautiously with gentle eyes and an outstretched hand. "Agent Smalldeano?" she asked hesitantly.

He nodded.

"Constable Quinlan with the Vancouver PD," she continued, offering a brusque handshake before bringing him up to speed. "We're just finishing the processing now, but here's the lowdown: Gunshot residue on the windowsill confirms our man here used the same type of firearm consistent with the bullet discovered at the scene across the street. Our guys did a height analysis and put him at just over 5'10", give or take an inch.

"The room was scoured clean, but we've got the witness out in the hall, along with the desk clerk who rented out the room to him a few days ago. We've also got a janitor who says he found three Molsen Golden bottles in a trash can down the hall; the can was in a 'staff only' broom closet and the only two up here last night were women, plus the only other two guests on the floor were women, so if the DNA in the bottles proves to be male, we're most likely looking at your suspect."

Vinny tried hard not to show the woman that his heart was racing, but he thought he saw a flicker of a smile pass across her pale but kind face and knew immediately that he'd failed.

"Come on," she said with a smile, "let's get you to your witnesses before you pass out from the excitement."

The desk clerk was a local teen with wide eyes and a wider mouth. She answered Vinny's questions perfunctorily and with a smile worthy of any top-notch customer service department.

"I only remember him because he asked for an upper floor," she was explaining as Vinny filled another page in his little black notebook. "There's a nursing home convention across the street this week—you know, lots of vendors for blood pressure cuffs and bed pans and whatnot—and so a lot of our guests wanted lower floors because they had charts, samples, displays, whatever to lug around each morning. A lot of them were also rooming together, bunking up to save costs, so he was my only single that whole shift."

Vinny nodded. "What shift was this? I mean, which night?"

"Three nights ago, sir."

Vinny looked into her eyes. "This seems like a busy hotel. Any particular reason, other than he was the only single to check in that night, that you remember him 72 hours later?"

He nodded knowingly as a blush rose from her chest into her throat and across her slightly puffy face. "Well, he was attractive, you know," she revealed. "Feathery hair, nicely dressed, sunglasses, straight white teeth. He looked like one of those kids on 90210, you know?"

"Kids?" Vinny asked, looking up from his notepad. "How old *was* this guy?"

"College age?" she guessed. "Anyways, a year or two older than me, and I'm 19. Turning twenty in December so, you know. Maybe 21. 22. 25 at most."

Vinny thought she must be missing something. He was new, sure, but he'd never met a killer younger than 33, let alone a highly-trained and deadly assassin able to navigate the globe undetected and circumnavigate three successful kills in as many weeks. "Did he hit on you? Make small talk?"

She blushed again. "No," she admitted, a little embarrassed. "I was kind of hoping he would—I'm between boyfriends, you know—but he was pretty businesslike. Most young guys checking in, they're with some young thing or checking out the local schools with their folks; they'll flirt anyway, ask you up to the room. I never go, of course, but they'll ask. Not this boy. It was just him, dressed casually, oh, and he had a golf bag with him, but when I asked him which course he was going to play he didn't answer but instead quickly changed the subject, asking if there was a fridge in the room."

Vinny knew what was probably in the golf bag. Their boy had used two different weapons so far, each one traced back to some local scumbag completely unrelated to each other. He was obviously traveling light, but had probably made a stop at a local contact and picked up the high-powered rifle that killed their latest victim.

"About the fridge," Vinny mentioned, steering her back into focus, "did you see anything on his person that might need to be refrigerated?" He was thinking of the beer bottles, but didn't want to lead her in any way.

"He had a six pack of beer. Molsens," she recalled proudly, earning an extra-wide grin from Vinny. Encouraged, she continued eagerly. "I noticed because a lot of Yanks do that, you know, they're in Canada so they think they should drink our beer. Kind of like us drinking Bud when we go across the border. It was all he had, in a white plastic bag like he bought it at the gas station up the street. I didn't see any chips, though. Or soda. Just beer."

"Cigarettes? Lighter?" he asked.

"Nope," she said. "Just the beer."

More nods from Vinny. He asked her if there was anything else and she shook her head. He asked the pale constable who'd made him smile before for a card and saw that her name was "Victoria." He told the girl to call her if she remembered anything, and thanked her for her time.

Next he turned to the woman in the short red dress. She had composed herself in the 24-hours it had taken Vinny to get to Canada and arrive at the crime scene, but perhaps that's because she'd been in custody the entire time. Thankfully the Canadian authorities had had the sense to book her on obvious prostitution charges, she had 3 grand and 12 condoms in her credit-card-sized purse, and was known to the local hoteliers by name. The police then hauled her to the scene for Vinny's interrogation.

"What made you return to the room?" he asked pointedly, using an entirely different tack than he had with the perky little desk clerk. She was old for a hooker, maybe in her mid-forties, but fit and firm and, if you didn't look too closely, quite attractive. "My notes say you finished your, uhhm, 'date' and returned to the room, letting yourself in the room with the key. Why so familiar?"

The hooker looked at him defiantly before admitting, "He hired me for the whole night. Said he was lonely, tired of sleeping alone. He sent me downstairs to the gas station around the corner for some milk and cookies—yeah, that's right, milk and cookies—and then said we could cuddle in bed for the rest of the night."

She fidgeted, her fingers aching for a smoke, and defended herself before continuing, "What the hell, right? The guy's paying a couple grand for the night. I'd rather earn it snuggling up with some in-room movies than flat on my back, know what I mean? Anyway, I got held up in the store and was just letting myself in the door when I saw this red, I dunno, light. Like one of those laser light things the kids use in the movie theaters to drive everyone crazy?

"I thought it was some fire alarm or something, what do I know, until it slowly crept down the wall and onto his forehead then, splat, his face splattered like a melon. Just like that. I dropped the milk and cookies and ran downstairs to let somebody know. The cops dragged me up here last night and asked me to show 'em where I thought the laser beam was coming from. I pointed up…here."

Vinny thanked her, nodded to Victoria and the two witnesses were led downstairs. The scenario fit. There was about five days between each kill, and Vinny surmised it was one day travel time for the shooter, three days surveillance time once he got into town, located the victim, and monitored his schedule, and then usually a day before the victim was discovered. Obviously, the shooter didn't count on the hooker coming back for a midnight snack and discovering the old man so soon.

Finally, Vinny'd caught a break.

Vinny watched as the Canadians bagged and tagged the beer bottles from the custodial closet trashcan, preparing them for delivery to the crime lab and a STAT analysis. His heart beat fast to think that they might make an identification, either through fingerprint analysis or DNA.

Sighing contentedly, he next looked at the list of business partners of SouthCom Digital, LLC he'd been keeping on the back flap of his little notebook:

- Philip Bronstein
- Arnold "Arnie" Kinsey
- Arthur P. Murray

Each bore a line through his name, leaving only two left on the otherwise blank page:

- Riley L. Quartermaine
- Arthur Ritchey

Neither name meant anything to him, though that last one sounded…oddly…familiar. He wondered if he hadn't heard it before, even recently, and wondered if it wasn't when he'd talked to Frank earlier that week.

Arthur.

Ritchey.

Nope. Nothing. Oh well, no rest for the wicked. He had to track down the next name on the list before he became, well, the next name on his list! There'd be plenty of time to talk to Frank from the Vancouver field office.

Maybe he could tell Vinny where he'd heard the name Arthur Ritchey before.

22

Moonglow Magnolia was down to the last few dollars of what she assumed would be her last check from Arthur Ritchey, ever, but she wasn't worried. Despite her name, Moonglow was no aging hippy chick.

She might have lived the bulk of her life in a cavernous trailer—and on a purposefully strict budget—but there'd been a method to her madness, and now she was enjoying the freedom of an unparalleled credit rating and the cutting of all ties.

Her little Hyundai had put plenty of miles between herself and that sagging trailer, and each one had left behind another layer of her former self. The few belongings she did bring along had been abandoned at this cheap hotel or that interstate rest stop along the way, until at last she was, quite literally, almost possession-free.

She had imagined the keepsakes and mementos would help her feel less lonely and at loose ends in her new life, but she'd found just the opposite to be true: The more she kept of her past, the more she feared her future.

Fear was something she'd lived with for far too long now, so she left behind the photo albums, the baby spoons, the matchbook collection, the movie stubs. By the time she entered Texas the car was all that remained of her previous life. Even her underwear and socks were new, charged at one department store or another along the way.

Her new clothes, her new shoes, her new hairdo, even the

new Mamas and Papas CD playing in the stereo—okay, so maybe there *was* a little hippy-chick left in her after all—reflected the roots of her new beginning. She had shed her skin, sloughed off the old her until only the new Moonglow remained.

If there had been an open courthouse along the way, she might even have changed her name, but she figured there was plenty of time for that once she landed. The change was tiring; each night she dropped into bed, dead asleep, rising bright and early the next morning to get on the road and keep moving, keep traveling, as eager to get as many miles between herself and Arthur Ritchey as possible.

As she entered the Lone Star State she smiled to think of the stack of credit cards lining her new billfold: 10 in all, carefully padded and paid off over the years, each with a current credit limit of $20,000. This in addition to the 50 grand she'd managed to save up over the years, pinching pennies here, squeezing nickels and dimes there, which was available as soon as she chose to break in the ATM card that had recently joined the rest of her plastic.

Yes, the old gal figured $250,000 was more than enough for a new start, particularly considering her low-maintenance existence and the fact that, no matter where she settled, she'd be getting a job for the first time in years. She didn't care what, or how, or when, only that the road in front of her was bright and wide and finally, at long last, free of obstacles or guilt or fear. She'd been ashamed and afraid for so long now. It was time to let the fear go.

23

The freelance killer stopped just past the Texas border, pulling his rented SUV into the first 24-hour, brightly-lit, cheesy-looking, souvenir-stuffed gas station parking lot he could find.

There was no reason to tail the shiny little economy car so closely anymore; The digital homing device his boss had installed just beneath the bumper several months earlier—gotta love those super secret spy shops popping up all over—assured the man he'd know just where to find his prey after he ran his little errand.

Inside the store he strode straight past the candy and snack aisles to the little area in the back where cheap Texas T-shirts hung—3 for $10.00—fighting Alamo figurines for space on dusty, crowded shelves. He ignored such commonalities and reached instead for the reason he'd entered the store in the first place: not to relieve his bladder or his thirst, but to add a tiny Texas spoon to his wife's collection back home.

Smiling, he strode confidently up to the sales clerk and rang up his purchase. Only three states remained to fill the US-shaped spoon cabinet he'd had specially-made for her on their twentieth anniversary, and with Texas added to the list now only two would remain.

Satisfied, he tucked his prize into the single piece of luggage in the rental car trunk. He'd once left a North Carolina spoon in the glove box and returned it with the car, so he'd had to wait until he got another gig in the state before he could replace it. Back on the road, he regarded the slim-cased GPS unit on the passenger seat, which was accurate down to the street name and, if need be, the parking space. He saw by the glowing green light representing his victim's car that she had stopped for the night. He wasn't surprised; if there was anything certain about this Moonglow character, she sure enough was a creature of habit. The man sighed contentedly and, using the sophisticated keypad, quickly calculated her position: the Greenbriar Motel, 4356 Old Dixie Highway.

Distance: 7.6 miles.

He started the car, put it in reverse, and was on the highway for less than 10 minutes when he found the Old Dixie Highway exit. Just as he suspected, it was another of those old-timey roadside inns the old gal favored. One story, 18 rooms, a numbered parking slot in front of each numbered door, an ice machine at the end of each of the two wings, motel office smack dab in the middle. Route 66, all the way.

For 72 hours he'd followed Moonglow Magnolia from state to state, rest stop to rest stop, drive-thru to drive-thru. Behind every hotel room he'd found a bag of trash she'd left behind, now carefully collected in his own trunk.

It was an odd assortment of do-dads, whatnots, and knickknacks. One bag held nothing but old plastic swizzle sticks from a few dozen Rat Pack-era cocktail lounges and other heartfelt memorabilia. Another held snapshots of the old gal sitting forlorn next to a birthday cake, all alone, year after year.

He knew not what it all meant, nor did he care. He was simply tidying up the paper trail, and knew his employer would want what he'd found, paying dearly—not to mention extra—for it when the job was done.

Along the way, she'd stopped at two similar hotels, always just off the highway, always on the main drag, always near a big department store where she'd walk just before dinner, returning home with tidy plastic bags full of new clothes and toiletries. Each night he'd rented the room next to hers, sleeping quietly in the knowledge, that by the time he did enter her room, she'd be completely unsuspecting.

Most people on the lam—and he'd dogged dozens of them over the years—were only nervous for the first 48 hours. They were cagey, looking over their shoulders, dyeing their hair, using cash, the old routine he suspected they'd learned from TV crime shows. A few states and 72 hours later, though, they started to let down their guard in a hurry: whipping out the credit cards, letting their hair dye wash out, growing back the beard, getting back into old, bad habits.

That's when he struck.

Old Moonglow was right on the money; her little silver Hyundai was parked in spot 6, right in front of room 6, and so he immediately asked for room 7 in the run-down front office. The room was like a carbon copy of the previous two she'd checked into, making him wonder if she was simply cheap or just nostalgic for easier, simpler, better times. He thought the latter, but not for too long.

He didn't enjoy killing women. That didn't stop him from doing it, of course, and the less he thought about her reasons for taking this retro trip to the West Coast the easier it would be to slip into her room and slit her throat later that night. So he stopped, stopped thinking about her altogether, and imagined his wife's spoon collection, and how happy she'd be when she finally added Texas to that big, empty spot on her spoon cabinet.

He smiled, looking at the clock. Moonglow liked getting

off the road before dark, so it was still early: 7:23 p.m. He wasn't hungry, wasn't tired, for he knew the job would be over soon and he'd be back on the road before you could say "Remember the Alamo." He settled back against the headboard of his squeaky single bed and waited for the night to fall. It would be here soon enough, and for that he smiled.

He just hoped Moonglow was enjoying her last sunset.

24

Frank Logan met Arthur Ritchey in the back of a legendary DC watering hole that was too obscure, not to mention too pricey, to make it onto most Beltway tourist maps. He'd made sure to arrive early, staving off the boredom, ennui and, yes, nervousness with a single vodka and tonic to steady himself before speaking with his richest, and only, client.

It didn't help.

He rose on unsteady legs to greet the billionaire when he walked in twenty minutes later and shook his hand a tad more firmly than he'd intended. As Ritchey sat down, Frank signaled to the waiter and listened patiently as Arthur ordered a twelve-year-old scotch, neat, in a slightly pandering voice that he no doubt used to speak to those less sophisticated than he. After the waiter had returned with their drinks, Frank nodded to his glass and sipped his new cocktail slowly.

"Thanks for meeting me here," Arthur Ritchey said after a sip of his own. "I know it's a tad inconvenient, but it's closer to my office and so much less, how shall I put it, claustrophobic than your digs across town. Wouldn't you agree?"

Frank, who was quite sure that Arthur Ritchey was a man who not only inconvenienced most of the people in his life but took great pleasure in doing so, took the casual approach to the dig instead, responding a little too jovially. "Hell, if I could work out of a pub, I would have hung my shingle out twenty years ago."

Ritchey nodded, unimpressed with Frank's working class hero humor, picked up his drink, sipped it smoothly, and set it back down again before regarding Frank with eyes both sharp and dull at the same time. "So, Frank, what do you have for me?"

Frank reveled in slowly, very slowly, taking both of his large hands off the bar and flipping them, palms up, in a gesture so obvious it caused Ritchey's eyes to widen. "I was just going to ask you the same thing," Frank replied after an appropriately uncomfortable silence.

In return, Arthur Ritchey cocked his head visibly, his sharp eyes never leaving Frank's. "I mean," Frank continued jovially, as if he'd just recounted Alex's location and the fact that he'd been recovered, safe and sound, "I asked you four days ago to see if you could find that missing diary and...."

"And I told you then as I'll remind you now," Ritchey spat, "I know of no such diary, despite whatever Alex's hooligan roommates told you."

"*Roommate*," Frank corrected pointedly, his voice growing as sharp and severe as it might have during an FBI interrogation. "He only had the one. The other person who told me about the diary was his girlfriend. You did know Alex had a girlfriend, right? And only *one* roommate?"

Frank watched as Arthur Ritchey forced himself to regain his composure. It was an awkward, if illuminating, moment or two. When he next spoke, Ritchey wore a smile as forced as the measured volume of his voice.

"I know you think I'm the typical workaholic dad, Frank, who's so clueless about his own children that he doesn't know whether his son has two roommates or three, or five girlfriends or six. I know that must fit conveniently in your single-minded cop's brain, and yet nothing could be further from the truth.

"I love my son, dearly. We communicate, constantly. I suppose I called his latest girlfriend his roommate as well because she was there so often. 'Mandy' was her name, was it not? At least that's what he called her to me. I hired you because I want you to find my son. Period. Not question me about mythical diaries or the number of roommates my son did or didn't have. It's been going on three weeks, Frank, and all you've done is spend my money and tell me things I already knew."

Arthur Ritchey stood up. "I suggest you start earning that money," he warned, "or I'll have to report you to the licensing bureau here in DC. As you well know, Mr. Logan, I'm a man of great influence and persuasion. If I tell them you deserve to keep your license, I'm entirely sure you will. If I warn them that you're undeserving, however…well, I'm sure you can always fall back on your writing."

With that, one of Washington's richest men pivoted on well-polished shoes and left the bar as quickly as he'd entered. Frank smiled at his retreating frame, as imposing from behind as he was from the front. It wasn't the threats that bothered Frank so much. It was the fact that his client had just lied to him.

Frank had agreed to the meeting not because he was eager to schlep all the way downtown and pay $12 for a mixed drink while he was interrogated about his progress in the Alex Ritchey case, but to at last confront his client about the missing diary. He'd been right to do so. The time for wearing kid gloves had come and gone.

It was only later, nursing his third drink, okay, his fourth, that the blood in Frank Logan's veins turned as cold and hollow as the melting ice in his vodka and tonic. Arthur Ritchey, a man so calm his employees had dubbed him the Ice Man, misspoke. Arthur Ritchey, a man so controlled he could visibly will himself calm, had shattered that serenity with one tiny word: children.

Alex Ritchey, it would seem, was not his father's only child.

25

Arthur Ritchey drove away from the DC watering hole fully aware that he might be tailed. He'd never taken a course on evading detection but even so he'd had enough common sense in his life to become a billionaire several times over, so he used some of it as he drove from downtown Washington toward the suburbs. He drove cautiously, but not overly so. Slowly, but not *too* slowly. He was a calm man by nature and even calmer during times of duress, so in this case he was *extremely* calm.

As he drove by his exclusive street without so much as a sideways glance, he headed instead toward the ritzy shopping plaza his wife often frequented, concocting a quick story—should he be stopped, though he had no reason to suspect he might be at this early stage—about buying her a bracelet she'd been admiring for weeks.

The story was a not so elaborate ruse; he merely wanted to pull into a parking lot and observe his surroundings. He did so, carefully. No one pulled in behind him, at least not for a few minutes, and when someone finally did it was a mini-van full of rotund honor students borrowing mom's car for a quick trip to the smoothie store. He watched them giggle as they spilled from the van like circus clowns, each one plumper than the next, God love 'em.

They made him smile, momentarily, as he got out of the car, leaving the keys in the ignition. As he called his driver from the men's room of the nearest bookstore, he deposited pages from Alex's journal in the wastebasket under the sink, making sure to cover it with several layers of sopping wet paper towels from the nearest dispenser. He deposited more while waiting on his man in the smoothie store, and more again in the jewelry store as he bought his wife a $5,000 bracelet he thought she might like.

When his chauffer pulled up in a taxi fifteen minutes later, he nodded curtly before taking his place in the hired yellow cab. He spent the rest of the afternoon at the movies, where he left a full quarter of Alex's diary in two separate men's rooms, and after that a crowded sports pub on the wrong side of town, where the rest of the diary was divided between a paper-towel littered trash can in the toilet and the dumpster out back. By the time he met his chauffer at a coffee shop later that night, the diary was done and gone. Hell, it might never have existed in the first place, as far as Arthur Ritchey—not to mention Frank Logan—was concerned.

He rode in the back of his car, smugly satisfied, and not bothered in the least by the fact that, before he'd ripped out the first twelve pages to throw away earlier that afternoon, he'd never even opened it before.

26

The Sniper felt comfortable being back in the States. He'd spent so long looking over his shoulder, studying Spanish to English and then French to English dictionaries and drinking first Guinness then Dos Equis then Molsens, that he'd stepped outside of himself for awhile.

Now, for the first time, he truly felt at home.

So, it would seem, did his latest victim: Riley L. Quartermaine. He alone of the four business partners—Ritchey was CEO and founding member, so didn't quite count—had chosen to hunker down in the States. He'd dug himself into a popular resort area along Virginia Beach and had done a fair job of camouflaging himself among the locals, sunburned and fleshy as they were. But not before constructing an elaborate ruse that had taken the Sniper to Europe and back again. Quartermaine had booked a flight and even rented a castle in the Irish moors, despite the fact that he'd never even left the country.

It had cost the Sniper four precious days to deconstruct the elaborate ruse; Quartermaine had even shipped ahead luggage and hired a full-time caretaker for the castle. Now for the first time the Sniper took his bead on a victim with anger and malice in his heart.

He blinked his eyes, twice, and pulled back from the scope before allowing himself to pull the trigger in haste. His training might not have been formal, but it was no less intense, and he'd long since discovered there was no use for emotion in any job. He blinked some more, counted to ten, and once again returned to his scope.

Quartermaine was there, sitting at his favorite wicker chair, reading some true crime novel he'd picked up in the resort's overpriced gift shop. The Sniper smirked. *True crime*, he thought to himself. *If he only knew*. Quartermaine's leathery skin looked tanned and relaxed, his face serene and peaceful. It ought to. For three days he'd done nothing but walk the beach and read, lie on the beach and read, drink and read, eat and read. Ah, the life of a runaway CEO.

The Sniper had to admit, it looked cozy. Maybe, when all this mess was said and done, he'd swing by a bookstore and hole up for a few weeks by himself and see what it felt like to turn his own mind off and step into someone else's for a change.

For now, though, work. He sighted his victim, the expensive scope revealing the wrinkles in the corners of his eyes and the hair in his nose. His eyes were dull and bright at the same time, his own life put on hold to escape into the pages of his beloved crime caper, be it a fictional one. The Sniper's finger felt smooth and cool upon the trigger; he watched Quartermaine's eyes move quickly as he flashed from sentence to sentence, line to line.

Then the eyes darted right, toward the front door, and the Sniper's heart fluttered as he squeezed the trigger, once, twice, as many times as the high-powered rifle would allow as his quarry swiveled on the chair and, suddenly, out of his sightline.

Still the Sniper fired, following his prey onto the floor and into the kitchen as there, just there, through the entrance from the living room to the foyer, he saw the front door burst open and a familiar face lunge through, his own gun drawn, FBI badge glinting in the Sniper's rifle sight. Time to go. This quarry was done; there was no hope of catching him now. He had to find his last victim before the Feds found him first.

Luckily, he knew just where to look.

27

Vinny kicked in the hotel room door just as the sound of the wicker chair splintering into a dozen pieces drowned out the screams of Riley L. Quartermaine as he instinctively dove to the floor. Had Vinny not knocked when he had, had Quartermaine not been distracted by the pounding on the door, who knows what might have happened?

There was no time for "if nots" or "what thens" for either Vinny *or* Quartermaine. He grabbed the older man and literally yanked him into the hallway of his sandy vacation rental, dragging him roughly along the hallway until the gleam of daylight was in sight.

There was no back-up or triage center for the two men to retreat to; Vinny was flying solo on this one, having just driven to Virginia Beach after landing at Dulles, all this after finding a dead end at Quartermaine's vacant Irish castle only 24 short hours earlier.

The jet lag he'd been feeling all the way to the shore was gone now, sucked down and spat out to make room for the jugs of adrenaline coursing through his veins. Vinny felt a tug in his shoulder as he hefted the larger, heavier man into the parking lot and against his rental car; he knew he'd torn something and there'd be hell to pay later.

He ignored the pain and shoved the shocked man into the backseat, spittle flying from his tense, white lips as he ordered the startled old geezer to, "Stay down! stay the fuck down!"

Vinny wheeled to a firing position, one knee under him for support, one hand under the other as a buttress for the recoil, visually scanning the perimeter for the Sniper. When the coast was clear, he slid from the passenger side to the driver's and started the car, gunning it in reverse and ripping off the bumper of some tourist's SUV in the process.

He ignored the scraping sound and slammed the car into drive, jutting forward like the virtual car in some teenager's video game, ignoring street signs and pedestrians as he careened into sparse late afternoon traffic and roared for freedom. He drove all-out for 5 straight minutes before he found a Mom and Pop gas station-slash-repair shop on the outskirts of town, where he pulled in behind a tower of tires to scan the perimeter once again.

No one followed him in; no one pulled in a few stores up the road, or down. Quartermaine was still hunched in the backseat, his large, fleshy body squeezed between one door and the other, but he wasn't making a peep. Almost as an afterthought, Vinny flashed him his badge. Quartermaine barely glanced at it.

The two were on the road, heading in the opposite direction, five minutes later. Only when they'd rented another car, only when they were halfway back to DC, only when Vinny had dialed three separate numbers to set up the safe house, only when both men could catch their breath, did Quartermaine dare to sit up.

"We're not out of the woods yet," Vinny said half-heartedly.

"Fuck it," said the older man. "I'd rather take one through the back of the head and die today then from scoliosis four years from now."

Vinny snorted. "You should be so lucky."

The men listened to each other breathe for a few minutes before Quartermaine finally regained his CEO composure and asked, "Who are you? What the fuck happened back there, and why is someone trying to kill me?"

Vinny's grimace didn't change as he said, "Mr. Quartermaine, my name is Agent Vinny Smalldeano of the International Elite task force, a branch of our federal government. *Your* federal government. During my investigation into the death of your three business partners, I learned that you might be next on the list. After tracking you down to Ireland, where you've obviously never been, I backtracked to find your resort here in Virginia Beach. Obviously, I wasn't alone. It is my belief that the same sniper who killed your three friends is after you."

Quartermaine didn't flinch as he asked, "*Which* three friends?"

Vinny didn't flinch either as he answered, "Let's just put it this way: you and Arthur Ritchey are the only two controlling partners of SouthCom Digital, LLC left alive."

Quartermaine nodded and, almost as an afterthought, added, "Thank you."

Vinny snorted, recalling the quick debriefing he'd had with Frank in transit. "Don't thank me. I'm the man who's taking you to a hidden safe house where you'll be handed over to the agents still investigating the disappearance of your business partner's son, Alex Ritchey."

"Shit," Quartermaine spat. "Why didn't you just let sleeping dogs lie and the Sniper kill me? Better dead than rotting in some federal prison for the rest of my life."

The two men's eyes met in the rearview mirror as they both realized the admission of culpability in the older man's statement at the same time. Vinny smiled despite himself. "I'd stay mute until we feel it's safe enough to let your lawyer know where you're staying."

Quartermaine nodded and followed Vinny's advice.

28

Dana checked her watch for the twelfth time in half as many minutes and watched the setting sun bleed through the drawn shades of Frank's outer office. She'd grown used to her boss's infrequent schedule, the comings, the goings, the never coming back, but ever since she'd begun to play a more active role in the Ritchey disappearance, she'd become more and more proprietary where Frank's time was concerned. She didn't know where he went off to when he needed to "sort things out," as he called it, but he'd been gone for over three hours now with no instructions as to whether she should stay or leave.

She'd left without his permission before, of course. If she waited for Frank to let her go each day she'd be there until he tripped over her on the way home, but with Moonglow's disappearance and his recent chat with Arthur Ritchey, things had started to heat up in the office, and his hours had been stranger than ever.

She knew her fiancé was at home waiting for her, eager to chime in with his complaints in favor of less time at the office and more time together or, barring that, at least a raise from the great and mighty Frank Logan. (She hadn't quite gotten around to telling him that Frank had already given her one.) It concerned her that she'd rather sit in the outer office listening to another Chris Botti horn solo or a John Coltraine dirge than drive home to hear her boyfriend bitch at her over Hamburger Helper, but not terribly so.

And that concerned her even more.

She sighed, switched on the lamp on the end table, the one they'd never used before a few weeks ago but now used more often than not as the nights grew longer and the mornings earlier, and regarded Frank's mail. She realized by the height of the stack in her in-box that she'd been neglecting her secretarial duties in lieu of her investigative ones, and now she sought to rectify that by attacking the envelopes large and small that had accumulated on one corner of her desk.

An hour later her desk was clearer and her trash can fuller, and she was finally ripping into the biggest envelope in her depleted pile. The big envelope, she knew held the weekly news stories Frank paid a local company to gather for him from every newspaper in the country. It was an expensive and daunting undertaking, and one that Dana was glad he hadn't passed on to her yet.

Apparently, Frank had been enlisting the help of the service for years, partly to supplant the meager budget afforded his department while he was at the FBI and later to look for subjects for future books. Lately, Frank had been too busy to look at the clippings, so Dana had just been filing them in one of the four empty file cabinets he'd had installed in her outer office.

She was going to do so that evening, but something made her sit back down and go through the pile personally. She wanted to help Frank, yes, but she didn't want to go home just yet, either. So she ditched her heels and planted her bare feet against the leather loveseat to dig in.

The clipping service organized their results by region, starting with the east coast and working their way west. An hour and twenty states later, she was thoroughly depressed. The daily crimes in DC were bad enough; to think that every city in every state suffered multiple murders daily turned her toes pale and her palms clammy.

By the time she got to Texas, Dana had almost become numbed to the death, murder, and mayhem—*almost*—but not so anesthetized that she missed one case in particular "...unidentified Caucasian female, 54 years of age, strangled to death in a roadside motel. Her only distinguishing feature was the crescent moon tattoo on her ankle."

Dana's breath caught as she looked inside her desk for the surveillance photos she took of Moonglow after their first encounter, less than a dozen quick snapshots from her disposable camera taken as Moonglow puttered about the yard. Her hands trembled as she rifled through the glossy stills, until at last she found the one she was looking for. It took a magnifying glass and three deep breaths but finally Dana could see the detail that stuck in her mind nearly a week later: the distinguishable crescent moon tattoo on Moonglow's ankle. The unidentified body in Texas had just been identified.

29

Frank Logan couldn't believe his tired old eyes when Vinny Smalldeano walked into the Krispy Kreme donut shop two blocks from FBI Headquarters. It was like seeing a ghost, and not just because old Vinny looked like shit.

"What the hell?" the former agent said as he nearly bounded from the booth where he'd been nursing a lukewarm cup of coffee and the second of his duo of glazed donuts. "I thought Flaherty had you circling the globe, chasing down some super sniper. Didn't sound like you'd be home for weeks. What happened?"

The two men hugged and Frank literally felt the relief pour from Vinny's veins. As he helped his former partner into the opposite side of the booth, Frank signaled the waitress for another round, and in seconds a steaming cup of coffee and two glazed donuts sat in front of Vinny's haggard face.

"I don't know how rock stars do it, Frank," Vinny said a few minutes later, after both donuts and a second cup of coffee were mixing nicely in his belly. "I feel like the lead character from some zombie movie. I just dropped a main suspect in the Alex Ritchey kidnapping off at a safe house about three blocks from here. About two seconds after I drove away, I realized I never even cuffed the man."

Frank would have chuckled, but now he was on red alert. "Did you say the Alex Ritchey kidnapping?" When Vinny nodded above his third cup of coffee, Frank said, "You *do* know I'm working with Arthur Ritchey to help find his son."

There was no irony in Vinny's voice as he asked rhetorically, "Why the hell do you think I'm here, Frank? Listen, I don't know what Arthur Ritchey's been telling you, but three of his business partners are dead, the fourth is currently in federal custody, and I'm still cleaning off gun residue from the Sniper's attempted hit on Riley L. Quartermaine."

"He's here?" Frank asked. "In the states?"

Vinny nodded, pushing away what was left of the coffee and licking the last of the donut glaze from his dirty fingers. He suddenly realized he couldn't remember the last time he'd taken a shower! "Best as I can figure it, shortly after Ritchey's kid went missing, his four business partners split for all four corners of the globe. At least, that was the plan.

"Turns out this group was about as fond of traveling as I am. The farthest any of them went was England, and Quartermaine never even dusted off his passport. He had this elaborate ruse of renting a castle in Ireland and even shipped a ton of empty luggage to himself there. But all the while he was holed up at some timeshare rental in Virginia Beach, of all places."

"Virginia Beach?" Frank interjected. "That's less than four hours from SouthCom Digital's corporate headquarters."

"SouthCom Digital? Hell, it's less than four hours from FBI headquarters. Listen, Frank, I'm here because Quartermaine's running scared. The guy just had four bullets pumped into his easy chair and three of his business partners are dead. The Feds are going to crack him, no doubt about it. The pieces of the puzzle are going to shake loose and we're going to find out who was, and who wasn't, involved."

Frank let the information settle over him, and Vinny waited a beat before adding, "Between you, me, and the hole in the wall, I think these four guys kidnapped Ritchey's kid. I think either Ritchey was involved and is killing his business partners to cover it up, or he wasn't involved but found out about it and is killing his partners for revenge. Either way, your man's next on our 'to do' list. If you can bring him to us, we'd appreciate it. If you can't, we're going to take him anyway."

Frank smiled. "So this was less of a reunion and more of a courtesy call."

Vinny frowned upon realizing that Frank was right. "I suppose," he admitted defensively.

Despite the fix Frank was in, he managed a smile to see his old partner having grown so proficient at the politics of the FBI. "I'll bring him in, Vinny. Just say when and where."

Vinny nodded and slipped the address of the safe house across the laminate table into Frank's waiting, if not quite trembling, fingers. "ASAP, Frank. ASAP."

"Understood," Frank said, nodding as he secreted the slip of paper into the hidden recesses of his wrinkled sports coat. "Listen, you look like shit. Can I give you a ride?"

Vinny smirked at the observation but shook his head nonetheless. "Tempting, Frank, but no. Flaherty's waiting in his office for a briefing. I'm already ten minutes late, but I couldn't see him without seeing you first."

Frank nodded in gratitude, watching as Vinny stood up from the table looking ten years older than the last time the two had met, and probably feeling twice as old as that. It was only when Vinny was halfway to the door that Frank remembered to ask, "Hey, Vin, how'd you know I'd be here."

"I'm the International Elite now, Frank," Vinny said with a crooked grin. "I know everything."

30

The records office of the Virginia Commonwealth, Birth Certificate Division, was as tidy as she'd expected, though not quite so large. Dana had envisioned something cavernous and sterile; what she got was a room both intimate and claustrophobic.

A clerk by the name of Dodie Hicks (really, Dodie Hicks) found the year and county in question, and then left her to it with no warning or instructions other than to remind her that copies were no longer a dime, as the outdated sign on the wall above the machine stated, but a quarter.

"Inflation," he said, shrugging, as he left her with the big dusty volume for which she had driven over two hours. She stared resolutely at twelve years' worth of birth records before any of them started to make sense. The codes, the columns, the certificate numbers—there was no uniformity, conformity or, for that matter, clarity. Although she had Alex Ritchey's birth date from the school records Frank had been able to obtain, cross-referencing them against original birth certificates proved more difficult than she'd at first imagined.

The clerk had informed her, almost gleefully, that two years after the date in question, all the records for the county had been computerized. Two years, and she could probably be pulling this stuff off the Internet with a social security number and Frank's American Express card, a frosty Mocha-chino at her side and the haunting smooth jazz to which Frank—and now she, too—was so addicted lilting in her ears.

Instead she crossed her eyes, sneezed for about the hundredth time, and finally, at long last, found the birth records for one Moonglow Harriet Magnolia. She was so happy she darted to the copier and ran off five copies before she actually sat down and read it. When she finally did, she had to go visit Dodie Hicks out in the reception area, where she found him hunched protectively over a tuna fish sandwich and bag of chips.

"Yes?" he said, perking up when he saw it was her. "Did you find what you were looking for?"

Dana thrust forward the photocopied birth certificate with trembling hands. "I think so," she murmured, "but I can't be sure. Can you translate this for me?"

He gave her a quizzical expression until she added, "The name I'm looking for is on here, see? Alex Xavier Magnolia, later changed legally to Alex Xavier Ritchey. But there's also another name right beneath it. See? I know Alex was adopted, so, could this have been his original name? Morgan Stanley Magnolia?"

Dodie put down his sandwich and regarded the form in earnest. He seemed relieved, judging from his expression, when he found the answer, getting tuna on her copy (luckily she had 4 more) when he pointed to the second name and said, "No, see? The date of birth is two minutes later. It's not the same child; this Moonglow woman apparently had twins."

Dana struggled to find her breath as she asked, "You mean to tell me that Alex Ritchey had a *brother*?"

31

Frank could have confronted Sylvia Ritchey in her sprawling manse, safe from the prying eyes of her fawning friends or the local press, but when he couldn't find her husband, Arthur, he tailed her to her favorite downtown restaurant, a snooty outdoors bistro bustling with plenty of well-heeled gossip mongers and roving eyes.

He parked across the street, pumping as many quarters as he could scrounge off his floorboard into the meter and letting her get comfortable. It was a crisp autumn afternoon and DC was ablaze in changing colors. Sylvia wore a sedate leather skirt, muted pumps, a cashmere sweater and a leather jacket. A scarf lingered gracefully around her dignified neck, her manicured nails fiddling with its fringe as she studied the menu, her well-coiffed hair barely stirring in the mid-afternoon breeze.

A handsome young waiter in blue jeans, a crisp white shirt, a tie featuring ketchup bottles and an apron turned down and tied around his waist took her order and returned quickly with a glass of red wine. Frank took note; it was probably time for him to stop drinking summer white.

When she had finished most of the wine, Frank crossed the busy Georgetown intersection and walked straight up to her table. By rights, she didn't have to speak to him. By rights, she could have called security, hell, even the police on him. By rights, she could have stood up, walked to her car, driven home, and lawyered up. But Frank wasn't interested in her rights and, as she eyed him coolly while he ordered them both another glass of wine, apparently she wasn't too bothered with them either.

"You look familiar," she said coyly, unafraid of this stranger who had just walked up to her table and offered himself a seat. He'd noticed that about the ultra rich; their world was so insular, so protected, so remote, so aloof, they truly didn't think anyone could harm them. "Didn't you do my husband's taxes last year?" she finally asked after eyeing him coolly for two full minutes.

Frank smiled, unaffected by the well-placed dig. "No, Mrs. Ritchey. I work for your husband in, well, in another capacity."

She nodded, acknowledging the waiter and accepting her glass of wine with a steady hand. "And what capacity would that be?" she asked Frank when the young server had left.

"He hired me to find your son," Frank said neutrally, watching as her expression remained unchanged.

"Ah," she said mildly, as if perhaps he had just suggested she try the butternut squash soup. "No wonder you look familiar. The FBI man turned author turned bounty hunter."

"Private eye, ma'am," Frank corrected her.

"Is there a difference?" she asked.

"Quite a bit," he explained.

She nodded noncommittally and sipped from her glass, apparently uninterested in further explanation. She dabbed at her thin lips with a napkin before asking, "You don't look like you're here with good news about my son, Mr. Logan."

"I wish I was, Mrs. Ritchey. In fact, I'm here for two reasons."

"The first one being?"

"Well, it's a funny thing but, ever since your husband hired me, he's been hounding me, day in, day out, for answers about your son. A few emails on Monday, a phone call on Tuesday, a visit on Wednesday, back to emails on Thursday, a quick catch-up call on Friday, then a few more emails waiting for me when I get in on Monday morning."

"What's so funny about that?"

"Well, Mrs. Ritchey, I haven't heard from your husband in two days, no one at his office will return my calls, and when I came by the house just now, your doorman threatened to call the police if I didn't vacate the property. So my first question, Mrs. Ritchey, is if you've seen your husband lately and, if so, where might I be able to locate him?"

"That sounds like two questions, actually, Mr. Logan, but, since I assume you're charging my husband for this visit, I'll answer them both anyway. First, no, I believe my husband is out of town. Second, since he's out of town frequently, I wouldn't have any idea where he might be."

"He hasn't called you from the road? Let you know where he might be in case anything happened?"

"Our son is missing, Mr. Logan. What else could possibly happen?"

"My point exactly, Mrs. Ritchey. Wouldn't you want to check in with him and see if there's any progress on the case?"

Sylvia Ritchey pegged Frank with a stern glare and asked icily, "Are you accusing me of being a bad mother, Mr. Logan?"

"Hardly," Frank replied just as icily. "I'm just trying to track down your husband and you were my first stop. Seems to me if my son was missing and my spouse had hired a private investigator to find him, I'd want to be in constant contact."

"Are you married, Mr. Logan?"

"No, ma'am."

"Have any children, Mr. Logan?"

"No, ma'am."

"Then how could you possibly imagine what you would or wouldn't do in my situation?"

Frank chose not to reply, inviting instead an uncomfortable silence. He sipped at his wine; she sipped at hers. Finally, she asked, "Didn't you have a second question, Mr. Logan?"

"I did, in fact, have a second question, Mrs. Ritchey. It concerns your son, Alex, and his real mother, a one Moonglow Harriet Magnolia. Would you care to explain any knowledge you might have of this woman? Where she might be located now? The financial arrangements involved in adopting your son? Anything, anything at all, along those lines?"

Sylvia Ritchey stared back at Frank with a bemused smile. She didn't flinch, blanch, or become sweaty. She looked, in fact, quite relieved. "My husband was quite wrong about you, Mr. Logan," she finally replied. "You're actually quite good at your job." She let the backhanded compliment marinate for awhile before she finally continued: "As a matter of fact, my son Alex *was* adopted. I do believe the woman's name was Moonglow something or other, but as you might imagine, my knowledge stops there."

"Of course it does," Frank said above the rim of the wineglass. They both knew she was lying, and Frank Logan wasn't leaving until she admitted the truth. "What concerns me about that statement, however, is the scenario I'm picturing in the delivery room. Alex's birth date was, what, 22 years ago? I think, if I recall correctly, August 12, 1983? So here's Moonglow, your surrogate, in a private room no doubt, away from prying eyes, your own nurses and obstetrician supervising the delivery, the proud adoptive mommy and daddy waiting in the delivery room.

"Early 80s, you're probably listening to Huey Lewis or Madonna, maybe even the Bangles on the Muzak while you're pacing in the waiting room. And then, suddenly, Moonglow pops out Alex, your fair-haired child, plump and pink, and no one could be happier. But, uh oh, hold on, here comes another baby. A twin? Yes, why yes it is, and yet, you and Arthur only take home one child that day. I'm wondering, Sylvia, if you could explain yourself. Enlighten me, if you would."

During Frank's recitation, Sylvia Ritchey' icy facade finally softened. She was far from broken, but Frank knew that somewhere far, far behind that frosty exterior something, somewhere, had cracked, like Humpty Dumpty, never to be put back together again.

Her voice remained even as she met his somewhat superior, self-satisfied smug tone word for word. "I'll enlighten you, Mr. Logan, because you've obviously done a fair bit of research. Likewise, I've done mine. The adoption was totally above board, as legal as a royal wedding. Back then, ultrasounds weren't what they are today; the doctors, fine as they were, missed the twin, and we'd contracted for only one child.

"When we learned there was a twin, we thought it best to let Moonglow keep the second child, a boy. We never knew his name, never saw his face, never heard from him or about him again. Any arrangements my husband made were with Moonglow herself."

Frank nodded. "Were you aware," he began, "that those arrangements consisted of a monthly stipend, paid to Moonglow until as recently as two weeks ago, when she suddenly disappeared? Were you aware that Moonglow recently met an untimely demise last week, and that foul play is suspected and, in fact, being investigated by authorities both here and in Texas? Were you aware that, if I don't find your husband, Mrs. Ritchey, the next viable suspect in Moonglow's murder becomes yourself? Barring all that, were you aware that the District of Columbia, this being the home to more politicians than preachers, carries stiff penalties for perjury, obstruction of justice, and aiding and abetting in murder for hire? Were you aware that I'm still a paid consultant for the Federal Bureau of Investigation, and that some of my part-time privileges include full protection under the law if I were to coordinate your arrest right now? Were you aware that, if you lie to me one more time, be it about your son, your husband, or the vintage of this fine red wine, I will arrest you, billions or no billions, and do everything in my power to see that you never enjoy another $14 glass of red wine again?"

Frank felt the moisture trickle from his armpits to his waistline, and was glad he'd chosen the summer weight sports coat for the meeting. Most of this threats were false, of course, but he suspected she didn't know that. Even if she had, he knew he could leave himself some wiggle room thanks to the fact that this was an ongoing investigation into an apparent kidnapping and that Alex's life might still be in danger. Frank had bluffed; Sylvia blinked.

"Rest assured my lawyer will be contacting you at his earliest convenience," Sylvia said coolly as she slipped a fifty dollar bill from her wallet and placed it between the ceramic salt and pepper shakers on the wicker and glass table. "However, I feel it is in my best interest, not to mention that of my son's, to be completely forthcoming at this, this...juncture. I did know Arthur paid Moonglow a stipend each month.

"I did know where she lived. I drove by once a month, if only to see if her son, if Alex's brother, was still around. I watched him grow up, that boy, in that scruffy little trailer park. I thought many times about telling Alex our secret but didn't. He loved us so much, and I didn't want to taint that love by admitting to him that we'd lied. I didn't know Moonglow had died; I'm sure Arthur had nothing to do with it. I do know where Arthur is, though I left the contact information at home. I don't know where Alex's twin is. He left home a few years ago, and I haven't seen him since. Believe me, Mr. Logan, that is all I know. That is *everything* I know. Now, if you'll excuse me, I must swing by my lawyer's office and tell him everything we've just discussed. Good day, sir."

With that, Sylvia Ritchey stood up on long, elegant, gym-shaped legs and strode away with a resolve as steady as her firm derriere. He let her go. He had more questions, but he'd seen the fear of self-protection in her eyes, and knew that she was telling the truth. Sylvia was by no means a dumb woman, but her husband was even less dumb. He would share with her what he had to, and only what he had to.

Obviously, arranging for Moonglow's death wasn't on that to-do list.

32

While Frank was busy grilling Mrs. Ritchey, Dana used the information on one of her photocopied birth certificates, as well as some phony press credentials Frank had lent her from one of his recent book tours, to do some background research on Alex Ritchey's twin brother, Morgan Stanley Magnolia.

It wasn't easy. Apparently, old Moonglow didn't think much of traditional schooling, so there were no preschool, daycare, elementary school, or even medical records for Morgan from birth through the age of twelve. Everywhere Dana searched, she came up empty. She started with the address of Moonglow's trailer park and moved outward, like a stone casting ripples in a pond, looking through the public records of every school, library, or walk-in clinic within a 100-mile radius. She finally ran across some short, clipped police reports of incidents that occurred during Morgan's "tween" years. Petty stuff, really. Pinching a candy bar from this convenience store, sneaking in the exit of that movie theater. Kids' stuff, really, but enough to get him pegged by the local law enforcement. Suddenly, when he turned thirteen, the trail got red hot.

Apparently Moonglow's lax mothering and lack of routine had a negative effect on little Morgan, whose acting out intensified to the point that he was finally sent to a nearby juvenile facility called, none too subtly, Teens in Crisis.

It was the late 90s, and, boot camps were all the rage, so

while the stint didn't show up on his official police record—it was a private facility contracted out through the juvenile court system—the name and address of the place showed up on a leniency plea Moonglow had made during his "voluntary incarceration," as the reports called it.

An hour later, Dana showed up at the facility, looking very official in her "go to court" dress, as Frank called it, a little black book in one hand and her bogus press credentials in the other. The place was twenty miles off the interstate, where the land was cheap and public scrutiny minimal at best. Her foreign car bounced up and down on the rutted road as she passed a band of scruffy teens in orange uniforms lazily tending rows of corn and alfalfa in the early morning dew. A bored supervisor blew a whistle as she passed, apparently to stop one of them from sodomizing his neighbor with a rusty hoe.

She parked in a half-empty lot and signed in at the front desk. The facility itself had the institutional feel of a public summer camp, though the locks and buzzers leading from the reception area to the boot camp proper were no laughing matter. She'd seen Moonglow's bills for this place and knew she'd spent a hefty chunk of her monthly stipend from Arthur Ritchey to keep his prodigal son here instead of in the nearby county jail.

Twenty minutes later, a plump PR person in polyester slacks and a sweat-stained cowboy shirt arrived to offer her a beefy hand ringed with sweat. "Phil Jackson," he said proudly, eyeing her up and down. "I'm what passes for a media liaison in these here parts, so if you'll follow me to the records room, I'll see what I can do to accommodate you. You spoke so quickly on the phone, I'm wondering if you wouldn't care to refresh my memory. What exactly did you want to know about Morgan?"

His voice was slightly nasal, and Dana had a feeling his southern accent was more for show than for real; still, his innocent sounding question had the sharp tone of accusation tacked on for good measure. He walked slowly, as if he might turn around at any minute if he didn't like her answer. "My paper is doing a puff piece on the effects of boot camps in the 90s. Apparently Morgan has disappeared, and we're using him to show how the minority, rather than the majority, don't benefit from such camps. Point, counterpoint stuff. You know, mostly for the appearance of journalistic pursuit rather than the pursuit itself. I assure you we won't name your facility and, of course, any information about you will remain completely confidential."

"Fine, fine," Phil said with a wave of his hand. Dana wondered why he'd asked in the first place if he wasn't interested in the answer, but she couldn't say she was displeased with the results. "You understand I wasn't here when the resident in question was incarcerated; signed on about three years ago, and I must say you're the first reporter we've had show up in person. Most of them phone in a request for a quick statistic or interview with our warden from time to time. I've asked one of Morgan's former instructors to meet us, if you don't mind."

Dana shrugged. "The more the merrier," she said, trying to sound as casual as possible.

Phil led her down an antiseptic hall lined alternately with inspirational posters—"A Book a Day Keeps Ignorance at Bay," "Smile! It'll Make People Wonder What You're Up To"—and handmade signs posting official rules: "Absolutely No Talking!", "Visiting Hours Are From 4-6 p.m., M-W-F."

The records room was a small broom closet lined with filing cabinets, the middle of which was occupied by a four-seater card table and three chairs. In one of them sat a firm-looking man with a buzz cut and tattoos creeping out from beneath the short sleeves of his predictably tight gray T-shirt.

He stood up when he heard the door open, and Dana noticed he clearly had to stop himself from saluting. He wore polished leather boots with long laces, tight sweatpants that left little to the imagination, and a whistle around his neck that hung halfway down to the Teens in Crisis logo on his T-shirt.

"Dana Patterson, meet Instructor Dan Higgins," Phil said as he made the introductions. He pointed to a slim file folder resting just so on the card table and then smiled at his colleague before adding, "Dan, I've got to make a call in the media center, if you don't mind. Just bring Ms. Patterson down with you when you two are done and I'll be glad to answer any follow-up questions she might have about the facility."

With that, Phil was off, and Dan offered her the seat across from him. "Morgan Stanley, huh?" he asked with a wry smile when Phil was out of earshot.

Dana smoothed her hemline as she sat down. "Morgan Stanley," she sighed. "Yes."

"He sure took a lot of flack for that name," Dan explained. "You know, the financial adviser? You wouldn't think our kind of clientele would pick up on stuff like that, but anything to use as ammunition in their ongoing war with the egos of their competitors."

Dana opened up her notebook and began jotting down notes. Dan sat up straight, prepared to be interviewed. "Exactly what is your 'kind of clientele,' Mr. Higgins?" she asked officially, softening him up before delivering the punch line.

"Call me Dan, please," he said with a wide smile full of crooked teeth. "And by 'clientele' I'm using a fancy term for scumbag. You can quote me on that if you want. Rich kids whose parents can afford to keep them out of jail…a bunch of snot-nosed brats, the entire lot of them. That's why I remember Morgan so clearly. He wasn't like the rest. Not as well-fed or well-bred, for that matter. Kind of scruffy-looking, and not on purpose like a lot of these goth punks we run across nowadays."

"Anything in that file worth looking at?" Dana asked, trying hard not to appear too eager.

"Help yourself," Dan said as he watched her flip it open. "Nothing but some test scores and his statistics on the firing range."

"Firing range?" she said as she looked quickly through the three sparse pages that made up the bulk of Morgan's personal file.

Dan looked at her quizzically. "Well, yeah," he grunted as politely as possible. "I mean, this is a mock military boot camp, Ms. Patterson. We treat it as such. These kids get plenty of discipline, PT, sleep in cots, wear uniforms, the whole nine yards. Archery, obstacle courses, reading a map…they get the full deal for their 2 grand a month."

"And that includes firing loaded weapons?"

He smiled again, seeming to enjoy her culture shock. "Yeah, as a matter of fact, it does. All under adult supervision, of course."

"And it doesn't bother you that these 'punks,' as you call them, are standing next to each other firing loaded guns? What if one of them got a wild hair and turned to the person next to him and blew him away?"

"Sounds like your classic win/win situation to me," Dan said without irony. "One punk's dead and the other gets a free pass straight to death row. Either way I'll never have to deal with them again."

Dana tried her best to smile but was finding it difficult to muster one in the face of such unbridled stupidity. She finally learned to translate Morgan's range scores and said with true admiration, "Looks like Morgan was quite the marksman."

Dan whistled through his teeth and said, "Damn straight. I'd never seen a boy take to firing a gun the way that one did. A real natural, and as a retired sniper instructor for the Marines, I can tell you I've seen my share of naturals. We kind of developed a bond, after his first day on the range. I kind of took him under my wing, I guess you could say. Showed him the fine art of marksmanship. How to align a sight, adjust for wind speed, which caliber was right for which target, you know. The basics. And then some."

She nodded, trying to dispel the creepy feeling Dan was giving off. At first she'd thought he was kind of handsome. Now she wondered how long it could be until she left the room. There was something dead behind the eyes there; something missing. To avoid eye contact, she buried her gaze in Morgan's file, where one word capped an otherwise stellar Teens in Crisis experience: AWOL.

She nodded toward the acronym and said, "Says here Morgan flew the coop. Care to elaborate?"

"I would if I could." Dan shrugged, regarding his watch as if he, too, couldn't wait to leave the room. "Trouble is, the kid just up and ran off one night. You've seen the facility; we're pretty low tech, and it was certainly no better 9 years ago. A kid wants to run off, all he's got to do is watch out for cow patties and corn stalks, maybe avoid a little barb wire, and if he doesn't mind a twenty-mile walk- he can be on the highway thumbing a ride to God knows where by sunup, just in time for the truckers to start fleeing the rest stops and heading for parts unknown."

"So Morgan just hit the bricks?"

Dan nodded, standing up. Apparently the interview was over. "We had a fine day, went to the range as usual, shot the hell out of a few targets, then it was time to report for dinner and time for him to go. He said 'goodnight' just like always, and that was that. The next day the cops were out here and I was hearing he hadn't been seen since lights out the night before."

She nodded, slipping Morgan's file onto the table. For a moment, Dan and Dana stood chest to chest in the tiny, claustrophobic room. They were about the same height, and he cocked his head to give her a queer look just before parting ways. "How did you know?" he asked cryptically before starting for the door.

"Know what?" she asked with a forced smile.

"The shooting range, the targets, the guns? How did you know Morgan took one with him when he flew the coop?"

"A gun?" Dana asked. "Morgan Magnolia took a *gun* with him when he escaped?"

"Not just *any* gun," Dan answered soberly, as if recalling the moment. "By now Morgan knew the difference between the second-hand rifles we bought half-price from the Army-Navy store in town and the good stuff; he also knew where to find our personal stashes, hidden here and there. Before he left, Morgan broke into the weapons locker and took...*my* gun."

33

Vinny Smalldeano watched with a slightly bemused expression as Frank Logan walked into their favorite donut shop nestled in the shadows of the nation's capital, surprised to see him accompanied by a leggy young companion. Not that Frank wasn't accustomed to leggy young companions, per se, but despite his legendary prowess with the opposite sex, he wasn't normally one to mix business with pleasure. At least, not in front of Vinny.

Vinny's old partner was dressed casually, in his trademark wrinkled sports coat and stonewash jeans, while his companion looked slightly more dressy, shapely and ripe in a form-fitting, knee-length skirt and turtleneck sweater that failed to hide the ripples of sassy young flesh that complimented her confident, stately stride. Hip-high boots gave her height and a fluidity that nearly left Frank in her wake.

The contrast was striking, and Vinny couldn't help but feel a twinge of regret for how the past year had treated his old partner. Once upon a time Vinny had been the bench-warming rookie, lapping up Frank's pearls of wisdoms as they chased down a demented serial killer cutting a swath through the south. At the time Frank had seemed impenetrable to danger, impervious to the winds of change, immune to his natural age; now he seemed like just another retired Fed, as handsome and charming as ever, but a tad rougher around the edges. Sadder, too.

Vinny put the brakes on the pity party and thought ruefully to himself that no matter how tired or sandbagged Frank looked at the moment, he was still the most cunning investigator on the planet. Perhaps the new, bedraggled persona was all part of the act. While he was still a Fed, Frank had played the steely-eyed, grizzled veteran to the hilt. Perhaps he'd grown tired of the stiff collars and stare downs, or maybe they just didn't plain cut it in the private sector. Maybe this new *Columbo* vibe was what it took to survive on the outside.

Frank made the awkward introductions while Vinny stood up, clumsily wiping glazed donut crumbs off on the hem of his own sports coat and smearing Dana's hands in the process. "It's so nice to meet you," she said finally, revealing small white teeth and a faintly southern accent. "Frank's talked so much about you, Vinny. I should say 'bragged' so much about you. I imagined you to be wearing a cape of some sort, maybe tights with a big red 'V' in the center of your chest."

Both men blushed as the three sat down. "Funny," Vinny replied, kicking Frank under the table, "he never mentioned his assistant was so young and, if you'll excuse me, so beautiful."

Now it was Dana's turn to blush. Vinny watched her with an admiring eye while Frank cleared his throat and corrected him. "Partner, Vinny," he said pointedly, causing a new shade of blush to wash over his companion's face. "Dana is my partner now. I brought her along because she's done a lot, well, I should say 'most' of the legwork on this case."

Vinny nodded, impressed. He knew from experience that Frank was none too quick to give a compliment. This glorified Gal Friday must be the real deal. "So fill me in," he said, motioning for the waitress. "Frank shared the broad strokes with me on the cell phone, but I'm eager to hear how you think our cases might be related."

He watched as Dana got herself comfortable, shifting in her seat and eyeing him tentatively. Next to her, Frank seemed content to listen: the proud father watching his daughter's piano recital. She launched in without prelude, either too nervous for the niceties or, as Vinny suspected, all too aware that time was of the essence if they were to find Arthur Ritchey and the Sniper still alive.

"22 years ago," she began, "Arthur Ritchey and his wife hired a surrogate mother to conceive for them a child, an heir to the already considerable Ritchey empire. Despite having the best doctors money could buy, the Ritchey's elite 'dream team' of obstetricians apparently failed to realize that the surrogate, one Moonglow Magnolia, was pregnant with twins.

"Although both babies were perfectly healthy at birth, Mrs. Ritchey decided that she only wanted one, that being the firstborn. She took him from Moonglow and named him Alex. The other she left behind with Moonglow, who named him Morgan, Morgan Stanley Magnolia, and raised him in a trailer park just a few hours from here."

Vinny had since whipped out his trademark little black notebook and was scribbling down the details when Dana passed him a single sheet of paper listing all of Morgan's vitals: birth date, social security number, last known address, various aliases, etc. He regarded it, impressed, as she continued. "Arthur Ritchey gave the surrogate a monthly stipend, generous by her standards, paltry by his, and the two brothers grew up independent of one another.

"Both Mr. and Mrs. Ritchey, if they can be believed, swear they never told Alex about his brother. Sadly, we never got the chance to ask Moonglow if she ever told Morgan about Alex. Shortly after he was kidnapped, Frank and I tracked Moonglow down and interviewed her. We didn't know then about Alex's twin. The day after our interview, she fled town. Later that same week, she turned up dead in some fleabag hotel just over the Texas state line. The identity of her killer remains a mystery.

"Concurrently, your sniper began eliminating American citizens residing in foreign countries. Though at first they appeared unrelated, it was later discovered that each of them had one thing in common: They were all CEOs at SouthCom Digital, LLC. Only two remain alive: Riley L. Quartermaine and Arthur Ritchey. Quartermaine, I believe, is currently in federal custody at an undisclosed location and Ritchey has gone AWOL. With me so far?"

Impressed or no, Vinny couldn't help but wonder where he fit into this highly interesting, if overly vague, puzzle. "Oh I'm with you," he blurted, a tad impatiently, "only I'm wondering if you're with *me*? How the hell does my sniper fit into all this?"

She nodded with a self-satisfied grin that was all too familiar. Glancing just to her right, Vinny was not surprised to see the same shit-eating grin spread across Frank's face. "Morgan Stanley Magnolia grew up to be one tough hombre. His poor mother, Moonglow, didn't know what to do with her fair-haired, wild-eyed child. Apparently, Morgan wasn't responding to all her peace, love, and incense.

"Not surprisingly, he ended up running afoul of the law and, after several stops in juvie, eventually wound up in a place called Teens in Crisis. It was a boot camp of sorts, plenty of strict discipline and salutes in the halls. There, among other things, Alex Ritchey's illegitimate brother trained with an ex-Marine Sharpshooter for some months until finally fleeing the facility with the Sharpshooter's personal rifle. He's been missing in action ever since."

Vinny stood up from the table; he'd heard enough. As he

threw down a crumpled ten dollar bill to cover the donuts and sped across the weathered linoleum toward the front door, he didn't care whether or not Frank and Dana followed but wasn't too surprised to find that they had. They stood facing each other over the top of Vinny's standard issue sedan, a Washington fall running brisk and chill through their exposed extremities.

"You're off to squeeze Quartermaine, right?" Frank asked, speaking for the first time since Dana began her enlightening soliloquy. "That means you believe us?"

"Hell yes," Vinny said, scrambling in his coat pocket for his keys.

"Any chance I could come along?" Frank asked, breaching protocol.

Vinny gave him a wry smile. Frank's resigned grimace said he already knew the answer, but he gave it anyway. "Sorry, pal. Current clearance only, you understand."

"Shit," Frank sighed. "That's fine, young gun. I've still got a few of the old guard in the Bureau who might let me upgrade my freelance status for one night. Hopefully, one of Arthur Ritchey's old haunts will pop up on my radar."

"Go ahead, Frank, and let's keep the lines of communication open. If what you guys found out is true, where we find one we're likely going to find the other. The Sniper hunts for two days and kills on the third. If we're lucky, he's still hunting your man. Between the three of us, we should be able to find one or the other."

Vinny paused, turned to address Dana, and smiled as he said, "Good work, kid. I just hope Frank's as proud of you as I am. Wish me luck!"

34

The Sniper finally tracked Arthur Ritchey down to a secluded office complex buried deep in some wide-ranging industrial park just outside of DC proper. It was a destination in the making, a bustling beehive of activity from 7 a.m. to 4 p.m. Monday through Friday, a virtual ghost town after that each weeknight, and all weekend long. When it came to hunkering down, Arthur Ritchey couldn't have found himself a better beehive.

The building in which he'd chosen to hide out was a cavernous expanse of rooms, some finished, some bare. It was a virtual maze of future cubbyholes, offices, closets, and restrooms, providing multiple escape routes for the prey and dozens of monkey wrenches thrown directly into the plans of the hunter.

Even so, there was good news for the Sniper. The number of supplies he'd hauled in so far, the leisure inherent in his pace, the resigned look on his rough, craggy face implied a hunkering down mentality. In his gut, the Sniper was sure that Arthur Ritchey was there for the duration.

It had taken an extra 48-hours' worth of checking bank records, blueprints, property taxes, and the like to find his busy bee, but the Sniper's industriousness—not to mention a sincere willingness to forego sleep—had finally paid off.

He'd arrived at his destination, weaponless, and worked a throwaway cell phone furiously for nearly 17 straight hours before finally getting in touch with a local dealer willing to provide him with a clean weapon at a reasonable price. Even so, it would still be another 48-72 hours before he could target Arthur with any kind of certainty.

For the first time in his career, he only hoped he could wait that long.

The other three—it had almost been four, until that damned Fed waded in, hero-like, and shot the plan to shit—were business; this was personal. He'd lost track of the times he'd killed this bastard in his head; lost count of the bullets he'd driven into his miserly old brain, again and again, night after night, year after year.

Thoughts of ending Ritchey's life drove him to distraction; he could already see that fat, bald head exploding into a thick puff of fine, pink mist, could already see the roughhewn drywall of the unfinished commercial building splattered with brain and bone, could already see the headless body slumping to the floor in a pile of blood and gruel.

Even so, the prey proved more elusive than he had expected. Ritchey was a businessman, a fat cat in an expensive suit, used to sitting on his haunches, not eluding an expertly trained marksmen. Still, glimpses of the old man had been few and far between. A flash of flesh as he skirted one window for another, a quick run to the back of his well-stocked SUV for more supplies. In and out, that was his style.

The Sniper realized that his old tactics wouldn't work. He couldn't set up shop from across the street and wait for Ritchey to run out to the car for more flashlight batteries or cans of Spam. His business partners, his fellow CEOs at SouthCom Digital, had been more predictable, less wary. They'd been on the run, sure, but they'd never really imagined a hunter on their trail.

When they turned their heads or craned their necks, they were looking for the law, some potbellied Federales or Canadian Mounties or, at the most, some shame-faced emissaries from the local embassy with their walking papers. They weren't looking for a hired gun, a paid assassin.

Ritchey was different. He seemed better equipped, more wary, and prepared to hunker down if need be until the heat died down. There was a wariness to his motions, an almost instinctual cringe that made him stick close to cover and rarely leave the shadows of his own making.

The Sniper was impressed, if undeterred. He knew everything about the man, and nowhere in his file did it indicate military training, covert operations, or, for that matter, a gym membership. So how the hell did he know to keep the lights off and his head down?

It mattered little. The Sniper was there to do a job, and he wouldn't leave until his mission was accomplished. He sighed, dividing his time between watching for his ever-elusive prey and looking at the custom-ordered, high-powered rifle he'd just bought on the DC black market. He'd been mistaken in ordering it so hastily; it no longer seemed the right weapon for the job.

He dialed his contact's number and asked him to find something smaller and lighter, silent but deadly. He was told where to meet, how much to bring, and how long it would be. Five hours. Not too bad. That left him plenty of time to pick up the weapon, familiarize himself with it, and leave his base of operations behind.

The job had changed; long range was too far away. For this job, he'd need to get up close and personal.

35

Riley L. Quartermaine looked across the table at his inquisitor and blinked into the harsh glare of a single desk lamp craned in his direction. *Shit*, he thought wryly to himself, mentally willing the drop of sweat threatening to leap from his furrowed brow onto the dust-covered interrogation table to stop. *They really do this shit. Just like on TV.*

The agent in charge, a smug, cocky young bastard named Smalldeano, had been hammering him hard for over two hours and was near the end of his rope. He'd come in all full of himself, barking orders and issuing threats and pacing up and down. From time to time he'd even come close to physical violence, but always the professional in him had backed down just before his fist, elbow, or thumb connected with this part of Quartermaine's body part or that.

Now Smalldeano sat quietly across from him, fuming, as Quartermaine circled around the subject yet again. He hoped the agent was comfortable; he'd been waiting there awhile. The way Quartermaine saw it, he had no reason to talk.

For starters, his business partners and co-conspirators were dead. The fourth was on the run, and if he knew Ritchey the way he thought he knew Ritchey, Quartermaine was sure the old buzzard would stay that way.

After all, he had the most to lose. It was his idea not to pay the ransom for his own son's life, his idea to wait his business partners out, his idea to meet at the abandoned warehouse and try to "reason with" his former business partners, his idea to threaten to expose them rather than save the life of his own son and, as far as anyone else knew, his finger that pulled the trigger.

And while it might have saved Quartermaine's skin to point the finger at Ritchey, that was only an avenue of last resort. What Vinny didn't know was that Quartermaine's role at SouthCom Digital had been purely negotiation-oriented. He wasn't a visionary like Ritchey or a numbers man like Bronstein or a financier like Kinsey or even a silent investor like Murray.

His sole skill was at sitting across a table from someone who wanted one thing and getting them to agree to another. He'd been doing it for over thirty years now, and he'd been doing it ever since Vinny Smalldeano sat across from him.

As far as he knew, he was doing it still.

His game plan had been simple: Smalldeano wanted Quartermaine to talk, Quartermaine would not talk. It was the opposite of what the agent wanted, and that was his sole job; to deny Smalldeano the satisfaction he so greatly desired. Quartermaine was in his element. Sure, the interrogation room wasn't quite the walnut-paneled boardroom he was used to negotiating in, but a table was a table, be it in the penthouse suite of some CEO's second or third residence or the underground bunker of some federal safe house. The basic laws of negotiation were the same: Deny the person on the other side of the table what they desire, even as you make them desire that which you wish. Simple.

Even as Quartermaine gloated about his performance thus far, however, he noted with a master negotiator's innate sixth sense that the mood in that tiny little interrogation room had shifted ever so slightly. The upper hand was up for grabs; it happened just like that.

Vinny Smalldeano reached across and turned off the harsh glare of the desk lamp. Then he stood from his chair, knocking it over. Finally, he reached under the table and, though Quartermaine couldn't see it, he heard the agent click off the digital tape recorder that had been running the length of the so-called interrogation.

Only then did Quartermaine begin to sweat.

"That desk lamp?" Vinny asked rhetorically, every syllable laced with venom as he righted his chair and sat back down. "Was a camera. That second click? A tape recorder. As far as I'm concerned, as far as the Federal Bureau of Investigation is concerned, this interview is over. The last thing anyone will hear is you, not me, standing up abruptly. Why, they'll even hear your wooden chair clattering to the floor. After that? Nothing but dead air.

"So now, old pal, it's just you and me. No video, no audio, not even a two-way mirror. Look around, chum. It's nothing but thick concrete walls and my ugly mug. Your lawyer's advised you to remain silent. So far it's worked. He's playing by the rules, you're playing by the rules, hell, even I've been playing by the rules so far. But your lawyer's strategy has only worked because he's playing the odds. More specifically, he's betting your silence will only result in a few days' detention for failure to cooperate or, if I can drum up enough hard evidence, a few months in a federal prison for obstruction of justice. Maybe a few years, considering this isn't just a federal investigation but an international one, seeing as how your business partners all wound up dead outside our national borders.

"Well, your lawyer's obviously never seen the inside of a federal prison. Then again, you're not likely to either. See, this case is personal to me. My first sniper, my first international case, my career on the line, so to speak. And me? Well, I care more about my career than just about anything else in this here world. So I'll turn off a camera here, a hidden mike there, and I'll beat the ever-loving shit out of your fat ass until you tell me what I want.

"That, or you'll stay strong and remain quiet. In which case I'll volunteer to drive you to prison myself, only we'll take a wrong turn somewhere and get stuck in the middle of crack town, where five gang bangers will put a cap in your ass, so to speak, saving me the trouble. On the other hand, we can avoid all the violence if you just tell me where the fuck Arthur Ritchey is most likely to be hanging out these days. Sounds like a simple enough choice to me."

Quartermaine looked at his interrogator and spat, "You're bluffing. It's 2006. Nobody's going to let you get away with that kind of cowboy bullshit in this day and age, least of all the federal government."

For the first time, Quartermaine heard Vinny Smalldeano's laughter. It was loud and raucous, and entirely sincere. This scared him more than the lack of audio and video recording systems. When Vinny stopped laughing, however, when the echoes of his voice faded from the room and they were left alone, stewing in their joined silence, Quartermaine really knew the meaning of the word "fear."

Vinny leered at him with a kind of youthful glee and stared pointedly at his hands, still shackled to the roughhewn table. "Let's see just how crafty one sincerely motivated federal agent can be, shall we?" With that, he clamped his left hand down on Quartermaine's forearm and used the other to plumb the back of his hand. Deft, nimble fingers probed deep until he located a vein amidst the soft, flabby flesh. This he pinched with an almost delicate care.

The pain started gradually, like a hollow thing; empty and

without teeth. Then it grew more maddening, suffocating, searing as the agent's two strong fingers moved next to a hidden nerve, small but excruciating, as the merest bit of pressure caused Quartermaine's knees to weaken and bladder to loosen. Sweat formed on the older man's forehead, then dripped into his wide-open eyes as the pain became increasingly uncomfortable. Quartermaine opened his mouth to scream but Vinny only saw the attempt as an invitation to apply more pressure.

A wave of nausea passed through his body, starting in his balls and stretching to his throat, where bile threatened to spill from between his clenched teeth. He didn't realize he'd passed out until he came to, minutes later, a grinning and serenely peaceful Vinny Smalldeano centimeters from his sweat-soaked face.

"That's just a taste of what I could do to you, Quartermaine, given the time and opportunity," Smalldeano all but bragged. Grabbing him by the back of his head, the federal agent forced him to look at the back of his hand, the source of all that pain. There was not a scratch visible, not a bump or a bruise or a speck of blood. "No evidence, mate," Smalldeano whispered. "Full of pain, free of marks. Now you're going to tell me what I want to know, or I'm going to spend the next three hours abusing the shit out of the rest of your 17 nerve junctions."

With that threat still hanging in the air, Quartermaine couldn't talk fast enough.

36

Arthur Ritchey sat in the dark. Quietly. And alone. He knew that was the only way to avoid detection, the only way to have fair warning if someone were to approach. His company, SouthCom Digital, LLC, had single-handedly helped move the emerging technology of digital communications—surveillance, detection, voice recognition, optical scanning, the works—from science fiction to commercial fact. And though he'd been far removed from the trenches of research and development for years now, decades even, he knew enough to realize that, with all that technology, all those heat-seeking scanners and enhanced microphones, in the end it all came down to sitting still and keeping your mouth shut.

So that's what he did. He moved little, surrounding himself with all the necessities: a stack of beef jerky and canned soups, water bottles to drink from, a spare empty to piss in. When he did move, it was rarely and only when supplies ran out or his sanity was threatened. Sitting for hours, alone and in the dark, was enough to stretch any man's capacity for rational thought.

He was glad he'd chosen this barren, unsophisticated, unfinished wasteland versus a more luxurious spot. With no air-conditioning, his body temperature was nearly that of his surroundings, making infrared detection little more than a minor concern. With no one to talk to, no cell phones or Blackberries or laptops to beep and ring and bong, the chances of alerting a voice-activated recording were nil. All in all, he'd chosen a tidy little space in which to hide.

Those quiet hours had been spent planning various escape routes. His current resting spot was central to several of his favorite ones, any of which would lead him deeper into the maze of wire-exposed offices and unpaved floors—and away from his captors. Should he be so lucky, that is.

He knew his greatest threat was not that of being captured by Frank Logan, the man he'd hired to find his long-dead son, or even Vinny Smalldeano, his former partner and the agent in charge of what the papers were now calling the Sightseeing Sniper.

Bronstein, Kinsey, and Murray were all confirmed dead. Quartermaine? He was likely dead or, worse, in police custody, where all kinds of horrid, rotting, stinking lies would spill forth from his ungrateful, disloyal mouth. Better he had been shot. At least that way, should he survive this ordeal, the last witness would have been silenced. Instead he was a wild card, plaguing him to the very end.

No, all he could do now was wait. Wait and see who was coming for him, and when. He had no idea who the Sightseeing Sniper might be. Bronstein's death had been a tragedy, but an anomaly. He'd muttered about it in the papers like everyone else, and though his hackles were raised, his suspicions were not. But when Kinsey was also shot, Ritchey was certain someone—or several someones—knew about Alex's death and were onto them, eliminating them one by one for God knows what reason.

He suspected it was money. Why not? They'd all been there, together, standing around like grinning idiots in a pissing contest, while his only son—well, not quite *only*—struggled and retched behind the locked doors of a stolen van. Perhaps whoever it was, the mythical "they," had even taken pictures, and were one by one tracking the founders of SouthCom Digital down to bribe them, blackmail them, only to kill them if and when their demands weren't met.

Farfetched and fictional, maybe. Then again, maybe not. Of course, it was not above the hit man he had hired to take care of Moonglow to do the job, but that seemed a little far-reaching for the high school dropout, ex-addict local man he'd paid $12,000 to do the deed. It had been hard enough for the poor fellow to make it all the way to Texas in one piece, let alone travel the globe setting up international hits. Besides, he'd had him killed two days after the deed was done.

No, he could think of no one interested enough in the intricacies of the petty jealousies of the SouthCom Digital founders or, for that matter, the well-being of his son, to take on the job of whacking four grown men who, among them, controlled the lion's share of the world's digital domain.

Even as he pondered the mystery of who was after him, he couldn't help but relive the event that had set this whole unfortunate business in motion. Oh, not the kidnapping of his son; that had been but a mere secondary explosion, a negotiating tool introduced by the masterful Riley L. Quartermaine. What was really at ground zero of the Sightseeing Sniper's vengeful antics was not a midnight kidnapping but instead a simple midday phone call from the head of SouthCom's leading rival, Global Communications Direct, or as they were known on Nasdaq, GCD.

It was well-known in certain circles—that being the small but growing billionaire's club—that not only was SouthCom Digital available, but she was downright ready to put out, to the highest bidder, of course. Years of infighting and insider trading had left Ritchey eager to rid himself of the SouthCom albatross, not to mention his quartet of greedy partners. So when GCD offered a cool $600 billion for the entire enterprise, with point percentages and annual salaries in the 8 figures for each of its founding members, Ritchey was eager to bite.

Not so his fellow CEOs. They threatened to break ranks, go to the press, alert the shareholders, etc., until Ritchey played his trump card and revealed through a certain legal loophole that he'd had controlling interest in SouthCom Digital all along. Red-faced, his partners could only slink away to their respective lawyers, looking for something, anything, that might tell them differently.

They didn't find it.

And so, the night before Arthur Ritchey was to announce that the GCD deal had been done, they had taken it upon themselves to kidnap his son. When the ransom demand had been the GCD contract, delivered in person by its crafter, Ritchey had all-too-willingly agreed to bring it by hand to their so-called "undisclosed" location. Armed with a small derringer he'd won in a poker game some years back and kept safely hidden from his wife ever since, he arrived with a blank sheet of paper in hand. Before revealing his pseudo contract to his foes, however, he demanded to see his son. "To make sure he's okay," Ritchey had begged.

Quartermaine, the brains behind the negotiating ploy, was all too happy to swing wide the van doors and reveal Alex, crumpled and exhausted, sweaty and rank, lying in his own piss and squirming against his blood-soaked bonds. He was doing him a favor, or so he rationalized, when he emptied the small two-shooter into Alex's brain.

Relieved of their bargaining chip, the four shocked kidnappers could hardly refuse to help Arthur bury his son in one of SouthCom's nearby construction projects. Two days after his son's death, Ritchey himself broke ground on the new project and watched gleefully as a fleet of trucks poured fresh concrete over his son's fresh grave. By now, Alex was resting peacefully beneath five feet of quick-dry cement, and three of the four men who knew his whereabouts were dead.

All he had to do now was survive. And, of course, kill the fourth.

37

Frank Logan felt awkward and off-balance as he strode purposefully down a generic hallway in FBI Headquarters. Six months of civilian life had left him spoiled and lazy; getting into his stiff suit and polished shoes earlier that same morning had been sheer torture. Still, the sacrifice had been worth the payoff, or at least would be if the files one of his old pals from the Bureau had promised him were waiting in Conference Room 9-A and held what he hoped they would.

The room, when he finally found it, was aglow with the brilliance of fluorescent overhead lighting and awash in the scent of a fresh pot of coffee. It made him smile to think old friends could give him such a warm reception, even if they weren't personally around to shake his hand or offer him an olive branch. Oh well, he couldn't blame them for wanting to steer clear. After all, his freelance clearance didn't exactly entitle him to trips to the 9th floor.

Still, it was after hours on a dark and dreary Tuesday, and the corridors had been empty of all but the most dutiful agents, their noses glued straight to their case files. Even if they did look up to spot Frank Logan—THE Frank Logan—strolling the halls, they would know it was with good reason and, for that matter, for the betterment of God and country.

And so it was that Frank sat alone at a conference table piled high with the financial records of SouthCom Digital, LLC. He was looking for something, anything, that might help him locate one Arthur P. Ritchey. He didn't know where he was looking, but he knew what he was looking for: a shell corporation with a local address, new construction under the SouthCom empire, a third, fourth, or even fifth residence, one the missus didn't know about...hell, even a local flophouse would do.

He didn't know where he was looking, but he knew he'd know it when he found it. After a few solid hours, he had a big stack of hell no's, a bigger stack of maybes, and an even bigger stack of could-bes. He started there, combing through all of SouthCom's considerable real estate holdings and marking them off, one by one. Too big, too small, too near, too far. There was no actual checklist, of course, just the mental one of a veteran Fed who had grown used to opening and closing the various file drawers of his own analytical mind.

He knew Arthur would want someplace off the beaten path, not a main SouthCom building but something in which they held a controlling interest; a remote office building or, barring that, one under construction. It couldn't be too visible, so the usual suspects wouldn't work there. It had to be off-limits, far from the prying eyes of average citizens or investigative journalists or even casual looky-loo's. Close enough to return from quickly and apologetically when the dust had settled, but convenient to several getaway points—interstates, access roads, airports—if the need to run should arise.

A quick check into Ritchey's banking records had revealed lots of recent activity, most of it offshore. There were too many accounts to flag, and, electronically anyway, Ritchey could move a vast fortune with the mere click or two of a mouse from a throwaway laptop, the kind his corporation gave away—in the tens of thousands, no less—as client Christmas gifts each year.

Frank shifted, then reshifted, then *re*-reshifted his piles until at last all that remained were a handful of potentials. On a laptop centered in the middle of the conference table, he compiled their addresses into a six-number database, then arranged them by location, including directions from an inter-agency map software program. This he printed, in color, from a copy machine two offices away and picked it up on his way downstairs.

It was just after midnight when he was through, and there were six addresses to check, all within a 50-mile radius. He rested his printout on the dashboard, nice and neat, and ordered fast food—complete with a XXL diet soda—at the nearest drive-thru on the way out of town.

He was 10 miles out before he thought to call Vinny.

38

Arthur Ritchey was a man unaccustomed to dining on processed sausage, but he couldn't help but think of his wife as he tore into his third cold meal of the day. Each year some distant aunt or cousin or nephew or some such relative sent them, via post, a half-pound tube of the stuff for Christmas. Granted, it was wrapped in the prettiest of packages and the liveliest of bows, but it was hard to dress up ground beef and fat encased in pig intestines. What was that saying about a silk purse and a sow's ear?

It made him nauseated just to down the stuff, but he'd seen it in the garage when he was getting ready to go on the run, and along with a Swiss Army Knife he kept in the glove box, it seemed like a good fit, so he'd grabbed it on impulse. In the end, it was about all he grabbed. Now the high fat content made his teeth slimy and his stomach rumble, but at least it kept him fed and he didn't need to light a fire or open a can to down the stuff.

He wondered if Sylvia missed him; wondered if he'd ever see her again. There had been bitterness between the two in the past—particularly over his continuing to send Moonglow her monthly stipend long after Alex's illegitimate brother was past his infancy—but she had always been true to him (even when he wasn't to her) and her sensibilities had been perfectly matched with his ever since they met at Dartmouth.

Even so, Alex's kidnapping had torn a vent in their relationship from which life-giving air had been seeping ever since. The delicacy that accompanied any twenty-plus-year marriage had turned downright brittle, and there was a hooded glare behind her eyes that haunted him, followed him, even when he was outside her cloying presence. And so he stayed away from her, preferring the office or the car or the gym or the steam baths than to standing too long in her penetrating, all-knowing gaze.

They had grown distant of late, and each day he stayed away only added to her suspicions, unspoken but present nonetheless. He knew that she knew he was involved, and worse yet *she* knew that he knew. The unspoken confirmation bent him in a way that made it seem impossible to ever stand up in her presence again, and he knew that no matter the outcome of his present situation—life or death, freedom or imprisonment—she would forever suspect the unspeakable: that a father could kill his own son.

As for himself, he was able to compartmentalize this fact to the point that, on a conscious level, it never quite happened. The images remained—his son's blood on his hands, the look of terror in Alex's eyes, the fear and pity on the faces of his former business partners—but those were mere fireflies in the deep, dark recesses of his lizard brain, the one that drew breath and pumped blood without him ever thinking about it or, for that matter, appreciating it. The walking him, the conscious him, rationalized the decision he had made, without perhaps owning up to it. He had murdered, but was not guilty. He was guilty, but not responsible.

Sad, perhaps, but not grief-stricken.

Now, of course, his lizard brain was on overdrive. He had to survive, first and foremost, before he could forgive his partners, his son, his cold, austere wife…himself. He knew that this ordeal was not the ultimate test, but that in fact survival would fit that bill.

Only in the quiet hours of his aftermath would the horrors of his past deeds come back to haunt him: deserting one son, killing the other, abandoning his wife, denying his culpability. The list of sins past, present, and future haunted him, but far from limiting his choices, they actually broadened his horizons. There was no redeeming him; therefore he could live out the rest of his days remorseless, sinless, and guiltless.

It appealed to him on a purely hedonistic level. He would be a man condemned, but freed of the normal constraints of polite society. Tipping, for instance, or holding the door open for little old ladies. Smiling, saying "thanks" or "please" or "sir" or "madam." The money at his fingertips would be considerable, his range of motion limited, but his future assured; he could live, would live, and there would be no looking back.

First: life. He finished his meal, regarded the remaining two or three inches of sausage, and felt his stomach turn over at the thought of subsisting another few days off of the slimy, warm meat byproduct. Ironically, he didn't think it would take that long. Arthur Ritchey was a man ruled by instinct, and now his gut was telling him the final confrontation would be soon.

Perhaps even immediate....

Outside the empty windows of the unfinished office complex where he had chosen to hide out—or make his last stand, depending on who came looking for him (and when)— he watched as the sun faded into the bleak, sterile horizon. He was not a man of great emotion or sentimentality, but he couldn't help but feel his hope drain away with the softening of the light. He dreaded spending another night in isolation, away from his 24-hour news channels and stock tickers and brandy snifters and three-piece suits and country club chums.

He knew instinctively as he leaned against the wall, an overcoat that had been folded carefully in his trunk his only pillow, that there would be no more cutting of the sausage or rising of the bile as he tried in vain to digest it.

No, he would sleep through the night and rise in the morning at first light, walking from the building and into his future. The weekend was almost over anyway; soon would come the workmen and the inconvenience of hiding in the recesses of the building for 8 hours until they left, taking with them their coarse language and ribald humor and fast food wrappers and career belches.

He faced the decision as he did all resolutions; resolutely. He would sleep, and rise, and walk away from the building with, quite literally, nothing but the coat on his back. (Well, that and several billion dollars stashed in a variety of offshore accounts.) He would not clean up his soda cans or sausage wrappers or throw away the discarded Gatorade bottles into which he'd been pissing for three days. He would simply sit up from his slumber, wipe the sleep from his eyes, take one last piss and step into—wait, quiet, what was *that*?

A sound alerted him to the presence of someone, or something, in one of the honeycombed cubicles several dozen yards away. Night sounds were not uncommon in the deserted, unfinished building; he had learned over the past 72 hours to differentiate between the heavy tread of raccoons and the scampering paws of rats, but this was neither. It was large, and stealthy, and unmistakably human.

He had gone into hiding, not search and destroy mode. There was no gun at his disposal, no hit man at his side, no booby traps set along the path to his secluded cubby, although God knows he'd had plenty of time to cook some up during his self-imposed exile.

Nor was there a lack of weaponry at his side, should he have chosen to feel a little more *McGuyver*-like. Mere feet away were nails and screws and screwdrivers and nail guns and industrial-strength staples and dozens of other untold, dangerous miscellany with which he surely could have done some type of harm.

But he never gave them a second thought; perhaps he didn't think his life was worth saving or, perhaps, that his adversary would prove to be that dangerous after all. As it stood, he had one set of nail clippers from his briefcase, the Swiss Army knife, and his own two, sausage-greasy hands with which to defend himself.

Arthur Ritchey was no judo instructor or survivalist—hell, he'd never even been in a barroom brawl—but his will to survive forced fear from his veins and alertness to jump to the forefront of his naturally keen senses. He recognized the sounds of stealth, but the fact that he recognized them proved that whoever—or whatever—was out there was far from stealthy.

By now the sun was entirely gone and darkness prevailed. Typically he enlisted the glow from a flashlight left behind by one of the workman at night, if only to help him direct the flow of his urine into a bottle or spotlight a rat in the middle of his tracks. Now he felt the darkness an ally, though he realized the sounds of his shoes on the unfinished cement floor was as bright a source of illumination as any light bulb, lamp or fire.

He crouched, cat-like, on popping ankles and already sore knees, the longest (though far from long) blade of the pocketknife extended and at the ready. He knew of no parrying blows or first strikes to disable whatever foe awaited him, only that he would lunge and take what he found when he found it.

He knew he could not outwit or outfight his adversary, but he hadn't survived this long to go down without a fight. He would accept pain as the tradeoff for his lack of experience in the fight game, but a blow or two here or there—even a bullet wound or slice from a knife—could not stop him from falling onto his would-be assassin with all his might, and hopefully doing critical damage in the process.

He was not a small man, and far from weak. Surely his physical stature, such as it was, counted for...*something*. Propelling himself forward would do plenty of damage on its own; using himself as a flesh and blood missile could at least stun, or perhaps even break, the body of his opponent....

There, there it was again! The crackling of a plastic sheet discarded on the floor and the scraping of heels against drywall dust in the dark. He kept his crouch, though by now his knees were on fire, and had at last managed to adjust his eyes to the dark when, all at once, the lights went on. All of them, it seemed, every last bleeding one.

And in walked a ghost.

39

Morgan Ritchey approached his father as unstealthily in these last few minutes of his life as he had approached dozens of victims stealthily over the course of his career. Career. He could hardly call it such; he'd been a volunteer killer, after all. Or, at best, a low-paid hit man. Years of life on the run had taught him the fine art of seduction, the ability to slip from one room to the next, the avoidance of detection, the beauty of violence.

When he'd gone AWOL from that horrid boot camp, he'd been forced to live a life of stealth, crime, and poverty. He could not return to Moonglow. Love her though he might, there were questions he needed to answer for himself, and freedom he required to find the solutions to his own problems.

The adjustment had been hard at first; homelessness was not as glamorous as it seemed in the movies and on TV. As plentiful as the predators had been back at boot camp, they were nothing compared to what he discovered living on the streets. Friends turned menacing in an instant, strangers violently surprising, and sleep became a thing of the past. He was forced to live with one eye open and the other on his backside, which seemed to be the only thing of value anyone wanted from him.

He avoided the traps of many male teens on the streets—selling their pale, emaciated bodies for drugs or food or scraps of cash—by becoming a human alley cat instead. He had formed no alliances, made no friends, and practiced safe sex whenever possible. He had one driving purpose—revenge—and it fueled his survival in ways no booze, drugs, or sex could ever touch.

When his trial by fire was complete, when he knew the backwoods of Virginia and the streets of DC better than any naturalist, crook, or cop, for that matter, he emerged from his smelly, shaggy, rough cocoon and learned to trade on his looks, his charm instead of his fists, anger, or violence. He learned where he could bathe freely, and stole only to feed his belly and clothe his body in what society deemed "normal." Those last few years on the streets he prided himself on looking better than most stockbrokers, let alone most teenage hustlers.

His hair was cut short each month, his face clean-shaven, his body pure of disease or blight or discoloration or disease. He ate just enough to keep his energy up, and well enough to keep his teeth clean and free of rot. When he at last walked into the campus library of some downtown community college or another, he looked more like a professor than a student, and even this helped him to adapt.

He stored his suits and ties away and affected the casual, even slovenly look of a street urchin once again. Only then did he fit in with the spoiled and ratty student body who frequented the library; only then was he allowed access (with the help of a stolen student ID card) to the stacks of magazines and microfiche files which he had so long coveted.

There he learned more about the man his mother had told him about years earlier—his father, Arthur P. Ritchey—than most likely the man knew about himself. Collaterally, he learned about the man's wife, Sylvia, and his son, Alex. Moonglow had been cryptic about Morgan's father, but mum on the subject of his brother. It was only when, during his research,

Morgan ran across Alex's birth date that it clicked: Alex *was* his brother; Mom had had two boys, not one, after all.

At first there had been a new source of violence, anger, and revenge. Morgan set about learning as much, if not more, about Alex as he had his father. He learned where he was going to school and tracked him there. He dogged his footsteps, spending countless hours on the fringes of this game of rugby or that double-date, this shopping spree or that concert.

By now Morgan's skills as a thief, burglar, and fencer of stolen goods was legendary, though few of the people he stole money from or sold items to knew of his proclivities with a gun. (Yet, anyway.) He used the proceeds from his ill-gotten gains to rent an off-campus apartment across from Alex's private school, and there he learned the difference between love and hate.

Alex had everything; Morgan had nothing. Yet they were brothers. The hardness of Morgan's features was reflected in the softness of Alex's. After watching him for months, Morgan had never seen his brother utter a cross word, strike a fellow human being, steal a taxi from another pedestrian, or even so much as frown. Even so, Morgan didn't think Alex's happiness came from his money, power, or prestige. Indeed, his friends were plain, ordinary kids from plain, ordinary families. His clothes were simple, his habits boringly predictable and considerably low-maintenance, and for the first time Morgan felt he was in the presence of someone truly...*truly*...kind. It was a word he didn't use often, but in this case it fit.

If only that kindness truly could have been contagious.

For months Morgan tailed Alex, literally living in his brother's shadow and haunting his every move. In a way, they were closer than most brothers. Morgan was there for Alex's first kiss, his first whiff of pot, his first sip of booze, his homecoming dance, his graduation; Arthur P. Ritchey, to no one's surprise, was markedly absent from these milestones.

When Alex went away to college after a few years, Morgan followed. He'd decided his revenge on his father—their father—could wait. Not only did he not want to rob Alex of his only male role model, such as it was, but he knew instinctively that his father's death would tarnish Alex's kindness. That kindness, that innate goodness, was the only thing keeping Morgan from truly crossing over to the dark side.

Even so, to keep up with Alex's lightness he was growing darker and darker by degrees. It was expensive to live so close to one of Virginia's priciest private colleges, and Alex's habits were such that tailing him meant constant expenditures on everything from swanky dinners to concert tickets to hotel rooms to rental cars for his sporadic but eventful road trips with friends.

He increased his criminal activity, and it was in the shadow of his brother's goodness that Morgan Stanley Ritchey finally committed the ultimate act of badness; he killed his first man at the age of 21, during a drug deal gone bad, and though the punk son of a bitch he wasted with a snub-nose revolver he'd stolen from a Georgetown brownstone months earlier would never be missed, so too would Morgan never be the same.

As his reputation grew, so did his restlessness. His pennyante crimes were bringing in less and less even as word of his savage misdeed grew and grew. Months after killing his first man, Morgan received money for killing his second. It was one low-life paying to have another low-life erased, and Morgan viewed it as business, nothing personal. He had come to believe that Alex had received all the goodness and he all the badness; he felt no guilt as his legend as a contract killer grew, until that one fateful night he returned from a job, only to find Alex's dorm room crawling with cops.

From the window of his one-bedroom loft across the street, Morgan watched through a stolen telescope as Alex's current girlfriend cried and his creepy roommate tried in vain to hide his own quiet tears. It wasn't until the next morning that he realized Alex had been kidnapped. The irony struck him like a sledgehammer: If only he'd concentrated on watching over Alex, protecting him, instead of trying to keep up with him, his brother would still be around.

Even as the cops bumbled their way through their own investigation, Morgan made it his life's goal to track down those who would rob him of his brother. The next day he talked to a neighbor who had seen a rented van just after midnight, another who had heard car doors slamming and muffled grunts minutes later. He tracked down the van, learned the identity of those who had rented it, learned the identity of those who had paid them to rent it, and then the identity of those who had paid *them*.

When the culprits proved to be Arthur Ritchey's business partners, Morgan broke into the office of county records and triangulated the location of SouthCom Digital's newest construction projects with Alex's campus dorm room. He found the van on the second try, but it was too late.

Alex was dead, and as he watched five men bury him—each with their hands on the controls of the cement truck, figuratively and literally—his rage knew no bounds. He could have, *should* have, silenced them right then and there, but even then he was so in control of his emotions that he knew it would be more painful for them, and vengeful for him, to hunt them down like the dogs that they were.

After they were gone, mistakenly celebrating their illusion

of freedom, he had dug up the body and replaced the half-hardened quick-dry cement. He had held his brother—touched his brother, talked to his brother, cried over his brother—for the first time, and then stashed his body someplace…safe.

Someplace…close.

Now he entered another of his father's abandoned buildings, another of his new construction projects. He walked clumsily through the front door, as big as life, and only began to hesitate when he located the warren in which his rat of a father had chosen to hide out. The old man heard him; that was good. That was all part of the plan. In his hand was a knife, a simple knife; nothing more, nothing less. Serrated, yes; sharp, of course. But simple. The boy who had become a man behind the trigger of a gun would make his final stand on the other side of a blade.

He knew it would not take much to surprise his father, and so when he saw the cluster of bright orange extension chords, the arteries all leading back to a generator behind the building, he chose to illuminate the final confrontation rather than slink up on his father in the dark.

He flipped the switch on half a dozen klieg lights and bathed the room where his father had been hiding out in a shower of hot, bright light. His father, cowering in a corner, pitifully clutching a penknife and rising on knees that he could hear pop from clear across the room, looked as if he'd seen a ghost.

Maybe, thought Morgan as he approached, *he had.*

40

Vinny eyed the vast expanse of gravel that stretched between his car and the hulk of building in which his quarry had only recently slunk and could think of no way to reduce the noise of his sneaker tread on the path. So he took off his shoes.

This was a desperate time calling for desperate measures. He slunk, service revolver in one hand and the laces of his dangling shoes in the other, sock-footed across a football field of white gravel that, for all the damage they did to his spoiled feet, might as well have been shards of broken glass. At one point the journey was so painful that he had to will himself to keep from biting his hand in place of crying out loud.

He moved purposefully forward instead, at last reaching a soft spot of grass that bordered the unfinished office complex. He had traveled through sunset, parking nearly a quarter-mile away in order to get the drop on the Sniper, aka Morgan Stanley Richey.

From his vantage point he watched as Morgan—every inch a Ritchey from the sprightly curls on his intelligent-looking head to the posture in his rigid, athletic body—stalk Arthur Ritchey, who, as far as Vinny knew, was under the watchful eye of Frank Logan. (Or at least better have been.)

Frank had finally called him on the way to the business park, and before they'd had to agree to a reluctant period of radio silence, his old partner had promised Vinny they'd each cover their assigned man: Vinny had the Sniper; Frank had

Ritchey. Vinny could only hope Frank was as dependable as a private eye as he'd been as a federal agent.

Vinny had tracked Morgan from his own hideout to Ritchey's, a distance of only several yards but offering a million different avenues for exposure to an experienced killer like the Sniper. Even so, the federal agent had a feeling the assassin had his mind on more than detection, so Vinny was able to follow his path with practice and precision. Now he shadowed the Sniper's steps, listening as he walked unabashedly through the front door and through the warren of half-a-dozen unfinished rooms to where Ritchey lurked, rat-like, at the end of the maze.

Momentarily dazed by the bright lights of the Sniper's impromptu illumination, Vinny crouched outside a glass-less window as at last the son confronted the father. Electricity filled the small but mostly empty room, and for once Vinny was torn between watching the fireworks and nabbing his serial killer.

Tense moments followed as Vinny felt emboldened to peer over the windowsill into the room. Ritchey stood on unsteady legs even as the Sniper paused, mid-stride, either unhinged by the sight of his father at long last or by calculation, striving to keep the old man off his game. For seconds an uncomfortable silence occupied every inch of the brightly-lit room, until at last Arthur Ritchey asked in a voice as clear and authoritative as if he was chairing one of his many board meetings, "Morgan?!"

The Sniper took one step forward even as Ritchey stood his ground. Vinny laced his shoes and bound them tightly; he wanted no loose ends or flopping strings to hold him back. As father and son squared off, he spied an empty tub of industrial-strength caulk, which he quietly overturned and moved closer. Knee-high, it would be his stepladder into the room if and when the need arose.

For now, shoes tied, gun drawn, one foot on the overturned barrel, the other ready to launch into action any minute, he watched from the sidelines as the Sniper lashed out at his father, berating him for the ruination of his own life and the loss of his brother's. Vinny's ears perked up; he knew Frank's case was a kidnapping and that it involved one of DC's, if not the country's, wealthiest businessmen, but could the prodigal son have information no one else did?

The father was not waiting to find out; he lunged for Morgan, knife drawn, but his footing was not as sure as his tight grip on the rage that launched him toward his only remaining son. Morgan easily sidestepped the older man even as Vinny leapt over the window and tumbled, face first, into the room. His tightly-tied shoelace had nonetheless caught on the rough-hewn windowsill and, thus impeded, Vinny had landed, dazed but uninjured, on the floor.

It was enough of a distraction for Morgan to pull the gun from his back belt loop and aim it at Vinny, the boy's eyes well-trained and alert as both pupil and pistol followed Vinny to a standing position. For his part, Arthur Ritchey stood trembling and cornered on one side of the room. His knife had clattered to the floor in the commotion, and lay there as impotent as the man himself.

Where the hell was Frank?!

"Agent Smalldeano?" Morgan said calmly, though the dazed agent noticed the gun never wavered as he spoke. "We meet at last."

"It's about time, Morgan," Vinny said, advancing by degrees as the gun remained trained on his head. Vinny's gun was likewise steady on Morgan's head. "We doing this the hard way or the easy way? Please say the easy way."

The Sniper didn't shake his head as he answered, "Sorry,

Vinny. You found me; that's going to have to be enough. I've got a little unfinished business here with the old man, and then I've got to go dig up my brother's body so Dad can spend the rest of his life behind bars. I wish I had time somewhere in there to make you the hero of the day, but right now I'm going to be a little selfish and take care of myself first."

From the shadows, Frank Logan emerged. Vinny breathed a sigh of relief, but not a very big one. Now Morgan would have to alternate between aiming his gun at Frank and/or Vinny, but the surprise also made the boy more jumpy, more unpredictable. Still, Vinny couldn't help but admit to being more than a little relieved that the old man had finally made his presence known.

"Alex Ritchey is dead?" Frank asked, gun drawn but pointed downward, as if to keep Morgan from feeling threatened. "Is that what you're saying, son?"

Morgan nodded. "Who the hell are you? Vinny's partner?"

Frank couldn't help but crack a smile. "He wishes. I'm his mentor, mostly, but in this case, I'm the man your dad over there hired to find your brother. You have proof of Alex's death?"

"Proof?" Morgan asked. "How about the poor kid's bullet-riddled body? But wait, you first: You mean to tell me that the old man actually had the gall to hire you to find his son's kidnappers, when all along he knew exactly who they were and, what's worse, knew that his son was dead?"

Vinny noticed a slight blush creep into Frank's face as he nodded in agreement. "Who killed Alex, Morgan? Do you know?"

Morgan glanced at his father, the gun never wavering from Vinny's face. "I can't be positive, but I did see Dad and his business partners all standing graveside as they poured fresh concrete over the poor kid. So if you can't get him for murder, you can at least get him on conspiracy, or aiding and abetting, or...."

"Like hell," came a cry of protest from Arthur Ritchey. "He's a damn liar and a charlatan to boot. I've never seen this kid in my life, and I certainly never...."

Arthur Ritchey's voice was silenced by a stiff pistol shot to the kneecap of his left leg. The puff of ozone that followed hung softly in the air as Frank and Vinny both rushed to intercept Morgan and his deadly weapon.

41

Frank felt the gunshot before he realized he'd been shot, and immediately decided—right then and there—to never go see a movie again. After all, in movies they lived on to fight another day, even ignoring two, three, four, a chest full of bullets to advance on their adversary and vanquish him, buckets of their own spilled blood at their feet and not a pause in their step as a result.

Real life was not quite so appealing. His hip felt on fire, and the slightest move sent splinters of shattered bone ever deeper into the flesh of his upper thigh and, God help him, lower ass. He'd managed to avoid gunplay in 92% of the cases he'd solved, and in all of those that had eluded him throughout his career. Even if he'd been shot on the job, at least he would have been entitled to benefits and advantages not afforded him in the private sector.

Leave it to him to receive his first bullet wound as a free agent!

The shootout had left him with a bullet in his ass and Vinny with a graze to the cheek. Great, Frank thought, one more beauty scar to add to the image of the dashing young hero! Meanwhile, Morgan Stanley Richey lay injured and bleeding—but very much alive—on the stark cement floor. Blood pooled around his neck, where a bullet from Vinny's gun, or possibly Frank's, had nicked something vital.

It was just as well, Frank figured as sirens approached and

Vinny continued to apply pressure to Frank's painful wound. As many people as he'd killed, he'd waste away in prison for the rest of his life anyway. Still, Frank fought through the pain to sidle over to the kid and ask him one final question: "Where's the body?"

Morgan fought through the unconsciousness that threatened to drag him forever away to shake his head. Frank fought through his own pain to kick the kid, kick him hard, as he spat: "You selfish little shit! You've wasted your life killing men, bad men, okay, but you made that choice. What choice did Alex get? To be adopted by a son of a bitch and abandoned by his older brother? Tell me where the fucking body is so we can at least give that poor kid a decent burial, maybe his mother some piece of mind. That's the least you can do."

Morgan's eyes rolled back in his head, but his lips struggled to move even as death threatened to overtake him. His hands slapped against his side and Frank thought they'd lost him. He was going into shock or seizure and it would be minutes before the paramedics tracked them down. But no, it wasn't his side he was slapping, after all, but his jeans pocket.

There would be no parting words for Morgan Ritchey, no dramatic soliloquies in death. He patted his pocket, once, twice, three times, then cough a wad of blood onto Frank's favorite sports coat and succumbed to the wounds left by Vinny's—or Frank's, there was always hope—gun.

Vinny spat, "Fuck," but Frank spat back, angered by frustration and hamstringed by pain.

"Check his fucking pockets, you impatient little shit!"

Despite the pooling blood and grim circumstances, Frank grinned as Vinny smirked. In Morgan's pocket was a map, the center of which featured a headstone bearing his brother's name.

Frank sighed in relief even as Vinny's face knotted in confusion. "What's the matter, kid?" he groaned as the pain threatened to sap his strength, not to mention his already short patience.

"My cartography may be off since I studied it in grad school, but if this map is correct, Alex Ritchey is buried smack dab in the middle of Centurion Center."

"The business complex on the Beltway?"

"Yeah, I mean, here's Dupont Circle and here's K Street and over here is...."

Frank couldn't resist stating the obvious. "Isn't that the corporate headquarters for SouthCom Digital?!"

And that was when the sound of a grown man pissing himself reminded the two that Arthur Ritchey was still very much alive.

42

Dana stood vigil at Frank's bedside, although he was well out of the woods by the time anyone at the hospital thought to leave a message on his office phone. It had been three hours since her fiancé dropped her off, none too happy as he sped away to spend a weekend with his mother. He'd told Dana she'd been "distracted lately," "obsessed with work, in general, and her boss, in particular" and that he needed a little, as he called it, "TLC." That he ran to his mother was the tipping point for young Dana.

As far as she was concerned, Mommy could have him.

Frank frowned at the story, even as he gripped her hand tightly. "You've got to think of your future," he said pointedly as she sat beside him, a cup of ice chips in one hand and Frank's big, bruised fingers in the other.

"This *is* my future," she said, nodding just as pointedly at the hospital room, featuring bouquets of flowers from dozens of Frank's fellow admirers, or her oversized purse, in which her cell phone kept buzzing as it rang constantly on vibrate mode. "*You* are my future," she added quietly even as the tears threatened to come once again.

She had been scared out of her gourd thinking of where Frank might have gone after their donut shop rendezvous with the hunky but unavailable Vinny, and the fear, loneliness, abandonment, and empty space outside her heart made her realize her true feelings for this man in bed beside her. When she finally learned he'd been hospitalized in "serious but stable" condition, she'd left her home and rushed to Frank's side, her soon-to-be marriage fading in the not-too-distant past.

Though Frank pooh-poohed the visit and scoffed at what he called her "fussing and carrying on," nurses later said it was the first time they'd seen color in "the old fart's face" since he'd arrived just the day before. Dana took it as the ultimate compliment, and about the only one she was going to get anytime soon.

Now Frank continued to pepper her with questions, even as agent Smalldeano hovered at the door, a weak smile on his face and the hovering look of concern behind his wide Italian eyes. "Frank," she answered for the twelfth time in half as many minutes, "Alex's body has been successfully recovered, the autopsy is being performed as we speak, and Arthur Ritchey's in federal custody awaiting arraignment on no less than two dozen charges."

Frank sighed, impatient with her recitation, but whenever she felt constricted by his severity or ready to flee the room for the relative safety of the cafeteria downstairs, or even the crowded gift shop, she stared sadly at the stainless steel cane upon which Frank would be dependent for the rest of his life.

Try as the doctors might, his hip replacement had been hampered by the bone shards, many of which still remained after this, his latest surgery. They had sliced skin, flesh, and the occasional nerve that left his left leg intact but painful to maneuver. So far he'd been out of bed three times, and the pain from walking across the room unassisted, at his own insistence, had left him pale, trembling, and shaken, lying in a heap halfway to the bathroom.

Dana felt sad, but not sorry, for the man. If anyone could triumph over adversity, it was Frank Logan. Now she listened as Vinny and Frank discussed various details of the case. She watched from a distance, letting Vinny take her place next to Frank's bed as she re-read the dozens of cards that accompanied the floral arrangements while keeping a watchful eye on Frank's expressive face. He tired so easily, and yet the old familiar gleam of a case in progress filled his eyes.

She smiled, nodded, and knew, hip or no hip, cane or no cane, he'd be back at his office before fall had merged with winter. She heard her phone vibrating against a compact mirror in her purse and imagined it to be one or another of the half-dozen news agencies calling for an interview. Frank Logan, it seemed, was no longer off the media radar.